PIERS TORDAY

THE FROZEN SEA

Quercus

QUERCUS CHILDREN'S BOOKS

First published in Great Britain in 2019 by Hodder and Stoughton
This edition published in 2020 by Hodder and Stoughton

3 5 7 9 10 8 6 4 2

Text copyright © Piers Torday, 2019
Illustration copyright © Ben Mantle, 2019

The moral right of the author has been asserted.

A CIP catalogue record for this book
is available from the British Library.

ISBN 978 1 78429 454 0

Printed and bound in Great Britain by Clays Ltd, Elcograf S.p.A.

The paper and board used in this book are made from
wood from responsible sources.

Quercus Children's Books
An imprint of Hachette Children's Group
Part of Hodder and Stoughton
Carmelite House
50 Victoria Embankment
London EC4Y 0DZ

An Hachette UK Company
www.hachette.co.uk

www.hachettechildrens.co.uk

To Star, who draws

'A book must be the axe for the frozen sea within us. That is my belief.'

Franz Kafka, letter (1904)

1984 Nov 19

Archive (TNA) (declassified 2019)

Further official records of the Prime Minister's
Office from 1984 have been released by the
National Archives. It was a busy time for the UK
government. Previously declassified papers deal
with many of the challenges faced, such as the
miners' strike and the IRA Brighton bombing. What
is not widely known, until now, is how the
government conspired to use the fallout from a
wartime scandal for its own ends.

Shortly after the end of the Second World War,
a secret government experiment exploring
unorthodox techniques to resolve human conflict
went wrong. Four children, Simon, Patricia,
Evelyn and Larry Hastings, had to be hospitalised,
and the scientist responsible, Professor Diana
Kelly, was removed from her post, charged and
imprisoned.

1

The children signed the Official Secrets Act and the site of the experiment (Barfield House in Wiltshire) was shut down. The matter was considered closed until 1984, when a chance discovery led to the explosive events related here.

Later that year, a classified file was passed to the PM by the security services, requesting her urgent attention. She wrote a note across the top.

'This government is for British jobs, opportunity and prosperity. We are not in the business of wasting precious resources looking for magicians, lost or otherwise.'

But then she read what was inside...

END SECURITY FILE

CHAPTER 1

Behind the Bike Sheds

It was a dull day in April and Jewel Hastings was crying behind the bike sheds of Eldon Hill School, which is in Newcastle upon Tyne. They had been bullying her. Again. These children were no better than anyone else. But they had somehow developed the notion that true happiness lay in feeling superior. So they spent a lot of time making as many other children feel inferior to them as they could.

Jewel Hastings didn't yet know that she wasn't inferior to anybody. In fact, even at the age of twelve, she was already one of the most remarkable people to have ever walked the earth.

How she discovered that is what this story is about.

All Jewel knew was that deep down she didn't know who she was, other than someone who often felt, just

as she did now, confused and unhappy.

She had said to her teacher, 'Why don't they like me? Why are they so mean all the time?'

Her teacher had nodded sympathetically. 'I think it would help if you appreciated that not everyone is at your level, Jewel.'

'My level?'

'All the tests show that you have far-above-average intelligence for a girl your age. Not to mention your vocabulary, the way you sometimes talk . . . no one likes being made to feel stupid, even if you aren't doing it on purpose.'

'Would you like me to use fewer long words?'

The teacher had just sighed, so Jewel went to the head teacher instead.

'Rest assured, we'll keep an eye on the situation. If your classmates pick on you again, we will take appropriate action.'

'What do you mean by appropriate action?'

He sighed, like her class teacher had, and pretended to stare at some papers on his desk. 'People who are different stand out, whether they want to or not. Perhaps you need to *adapt*.'

It was no easier talking to her adoptive mother, Patricia.

4

'Patricia,' (which was what she always called her) Jewel said one evening, when they were standing next to each other at the kitchen sink, washing and drying dishes, 'everyone at school thinks I'm a nerd. Do you think I'm a nerd?'

Patricia let the plate she was washing slip silently into the water. She laid down her brush and peeled off her gloves. Turning to face Jewel, she gave her an unexpectedly long and deep hug.

'My precious Jewel. You are just that, precious. Not a nerd, not strange, not weird, but precious and brilliant – and most importantly of all, you are you, and never apologise for that.'

As the words poured over her, Jewel shrank away inside. This was all too much. She didn't want to make a fuss. What did she mean, 'you are you'? That would be easier if she knew who she actually was.

Patricia Hastings had raised her since she was a baby girl. Jewel didn't know who her birth mother or father were, or even whether they were still alive. In a way, that didn't matter, because Patricia loved her as much as any mum could. Although perhaps, sometimes, just a bit too much.

She picked up the tea towel again. 'Don't worry. I'm

probably just imagining it. I'm all right.'

Except she wasn't.

'I don't get it,' she said to herself later in bed. 'They tell you at school to be curious about things and work out how they work, and then when you do, everyone else turns on you. Am I that different to anyone else?'

Perhaps she was.

But just how different, she did not yet know.

Which was why on this warm but cloudy day in April, Jewel was sitting on the ground with her back against the bike sheds, looking at the ground – littered with pink splodges of Hubba Bubba bubblegum – and feeling very alone.

Although, she wasn't entirely alone.

From her school blazer, an urgent voice demanded her attention. Her jacket pocket bulged and wriggled, clawing at her hip, and a volley of squeaks from inside pushed all other thoughts aside.

'I'm coming,' said Jewel, as she scooped a furry package out from a nest of damp wood shavings and tissue paper concealed in her pocket. The furry package immediately nipped her before peeing everywhere then cuddling up in the crook of her arm, as if that was normal and acceptable behaviour.

'Hello Fizz,' said Jewel, wiping the tears from her face. 'You don't think I'm a nerd, do you, little one?'

That was unclear. Not much was known about her hamster's ability to think about anything, but he most definitely liked to make a lot of noise. He chattered, squeaked, shrieked, scratched, hissed, snored and generally made more of a hullabaloo than your average jungle at dawn. He was named Fizz, after Fizzgig in *The Dark Crystal*, one of Jewel's favourite films.

Fizz made a noise that sounded like an angry hairbrush exploding, and then he bit her ear.

'That is consistent with your previously expressed opinion,' noted Jewel, firmly but gently removing the hamster from her left earlobe.

The hamster squeaked some more.

'I wish I could speak hamster,' she said. 'No one could describe those squeaks as nice, but I believe their meaning might be.'

Fizz's endless squeaking was making her feel better, as it often did, and she could have stayed exactly where she was for quite some time longer had there not been a cry from behind her.

'Here she is!'

It was not a nice voice.

'Nerd brain! You can run but you can't hide!' said another voice, sounding no nicer.

'Look, she's brought her pet rat into school!' said another, lunging for Fizz. He dangled the hamster upside down by its stubby tail. Fizz was squealing, jerking from side to side in distress.

'Leave him alone!' yelled Jewel. 'What did he ever do to you?'

The boy walked over to the rusting bin by the bike shed and kicked off the lid with a clatter. He dangled her pet over the mound of rotten food and rubbish steaming inside.

Jewel scrambled to her feet.

'Don't you dare!'

'Do you know what rats are good for, weirdo?'

And something flipped inside Jewel. Not rage, but a burst of white light, knowledge that she didn't know she possessed, shot to the front of her mind with unexpected speed.

'Yes. Rats are scavengers who dispose of waste, and are a rich food source for predators such as owls and foxes.'

Often Jewel knew things without knowing quite why she did. But she had clearly read about rats somewhere, or watched a wildlife documentary on TV. The boy smirked at her. 'Whatever, brainbox. You're such a weirdo.'

Right on cue, Fizz jerked up and nipped his finger, sending him tumbling back into the bin with a yelp, while Fizz scarpered off down his flailing arms and legs.

Jewel carefully picked him up. 'But this is a hamster. And hamsters are good for biting bullies.'

The other children froze for a moment, which was just long enough for Jewel. She sprinted for the open gates, skidding across the yard. Parents were gathering, their cars squeezed along the narrow road overhung by beech trees. There was a low murmur of greetings, and an atmosphere of friendliness, as the school day drew to a close, and the warmth of home once more beckoned.

Jewel relaxed for a moment.

Then she heard the cries.

They were still coming, thundering after her. Just three or four, but that was enough.

She had to get away, and fast, to somewhere safe. Home was not safe. Some of them knew where she lived and were capable of making nice and smiling politely to get through the front door, but as soon as her mother's back was turned . . .

'Hold on tight, Fizz . . .' Jewel took a sudden corner, careering into the next street.

Fizz squealed a reply that suggested he hadn't heard

9

the instruction quite in time.

His owner kept running as fast as she could, feeling like she was running for her life, constantly turning her head over her shoulder to see if they were still in pursuit, and they were. Her chest pumped and her face felt hot. She had to find somewhere to hide before she ran out of steam.

The library? She glanced down at her digital Casio watch and then remembered that it now shut early on Wednesdays. Something to do with the new government, her mum had said. She kept on running, into the main high street now, past the Our Price record store and Ratner's the jewellers, past the Safeway supermarket, WHSmith, Marks & Spencer, a Wimpy burger bar . . .

And now it had started to rain. An April shower that darkened the day and spotted the pavement. In a matter of minutes it had become a storm, sending everyone in search of doorways and bus shelters to hide from the downpour.

Fizz made a repeated noise that sounded like a wet dog climbing out of a river.

'I heard you the first time, thank you,' said Jewel. 'Let's find somewhere to dry you off.'

It was raining so hard that Jewel nearly ran straight past the bookshop. There was no sign and the faded canvas awning over the window cast the whole front into shadow. But something made her stop, as if a voice had called out her name.

Except it hadn't. At least, none that she could hear.

Now heaving for breath, she took cover under the awning, only to find it was full of holes and that water continued to drip on to her head and shoulders. Glancing up, she saw that there had once been a name on the cracked wooden sign above the window, but it was so faded she could only make out a few barely legible letters.

B ARF EL
BO KS

She couldn't remember seeing the shop before.

The books that were on display, heavy volumes arranged on plinths covered in dusty black cloth, were not any that she recognised, and certainly not any that appealed. These were almost the worst kind of books. Her face pressed against the glass, she could just make out the covers and the strange, archaic lettering in gold which adorned them and which also made no sense to her at all.

'I don't suppose you read Latin, do you Fizz?'

Fizz made his general feelings on Latin and whether

hamsters should be able to read it abundantly clear. These were not, overall, very positive.

Jewel glanced back up the street. The gang's path was blocked by huddles of shoppers searching for umbrellas, the sheets of rain slicing the air.

She took her chance and pushed the door open, barely noticing the strange carvings which adorned its ancient wooden panels, only registering that something made of such blackened wood looked as old as the books on the plinths. An antique bell tinkled loudly above her head, to which Fizz burbled a reply.

Ducking down behind the plinths, she heard shouts of fury as her pursuers ran straight past the shop.

'We'll be safe here for now, Fizz,' she said. '*They* have not previously shown much interest in bookshops.'

Her hamster snorted in agreement, although it wasn't clear how much he was into bookshops either. Collapsing to the floor, her back to the window, Jewel checked her watch again.

'It's exactly 16:08. We should stay here until we're one hundred per cent sure that they've gone.'

Fizz clambered out of her pocket and began to clean his face more angrily than Jewel had ever seen anyone clean their face in her life. The hamster then scurried down her pleated grey school skirt to explore the shop floor.

'Fizz!' she hissed. 'Come back here at once! I'm sure we're not allowed to . . .'

Her pet stopped, turned, looked at her, and made a noise so rude that even the books blushed.

'And that's definitely not allowed!'

But he just carried on, disappearing amongst the aisles of gloomy shelves.

There wasn't much sign of light or life in the shop. The place smelled of rough paper edges and old shoes, just like her mum's study, so she felt quite at home. She wondered where the shopkeeper was and whether Fizz was going to get her in trouble.

Again.

'Hello?' she called out. 'I'm sorry about the hamster, but he's naturally stubborn.'

Perhaps the owner had popped out for a moment. Driven by sheer curiosity, as well as a duty to keep an eye on Fizz, Jewel picked herself up, and stepped further in.

A floorboard gave a warning crack.

Jewel tried to ignore her heart hammering against her chest, and began to browse the shelves. She didn't know exactly what she was looking for, which is – of course – the

13

point of bookshops. She just felt that when she saw it, she would know.

It was now so dark with rain clouds outside that it was getting hard to see inside.

Surely if the shop had been left open, the absent owner wouldn't mind if she turned a light on? She ran her hand blindly over the wall by the door till she felt a satisfyingly old switch. A series of low hanging lamps dangling in between the bookcases flickered on, casting dim pools of light over the dust-carpeted floorboards.

Fizz perched halfway up one such shelf, happily munching his way through *A Guide to Hungarian Grammar*. Perhaps no one would mind. These books were old. The lettering on the spines was so worn and hard to read in the light that she often had to open a book and turn a few of the fragile pages to find out the title.

A sudden noise broke Jewel's reverie, making her start.

The strangest sound, a kind of riffling in the air, as if someone had turned on an overhead fan. A definite change in the pressure, which she sensed on her skin.

'Who's there?' she said, but there was no reply. She hadn't heard either the door open or the bell ring.

Jewel felt a chill on the back of her neck. She had heard something; she wasn't imagining it. From the row of shelves beyond, she thought she heard a floorboard creak. It wasn't Fizz, who was now on the shelf just by her left ear, chewing through *A Short History of the Turnip*.

'I'm not afraid, whoever you are!' she lied. There was another creak from the other side. She closed her eyes and listened. Even Fizz went deadly quiet, which never happened. Was that breathing?

There was only one way to find out.

Stepping gingerly, she emerged around the corner of the bookcase, and walked straight into one of the low hanging lights, cracking her forehead on the metal helmet shade.

She cried out.

The lamp swung giddily between the shelves, flinging an erratic spotlight up and down the aisle.

On the top row.

On the bottom corner of the bookcase.

And on the large book, just lying there in the middle of the floor.

The book was an atlas.

That wasn't unusual. Being a geography professor, Patricia had lots of those at home, if not as old as this one.

This atlas, though, was of a place Jewel had never heard of before.

A place called Folio.

CHAPTER 2

What Jewel Did Next

Jewel hadn't heard the atlas fall from anywhere, and it was not the kind of book to fall without a sound. It was about twice the size of a Yellow Pages telephone directory, and looked heavy. She had only been browsing in this aisle of shelves a moment ago, and she could have sworn there was no book on the floor before. Had someone put it there?

She crouched down to take a closer look. With a sharp breath, she blew some of the dust off the heavy leather cover. By tracing the engraved gold lettering with her finger, she was able to decipher some of the words. The rest of the title was in Latin, so it was difficult. Fizz climbed on her shoulder to take a better look, but judging by his muttered chirrups of disgust, he could make no more sense of it than she could.

'Fizz,' said Jewel calmly. 'I've told you before. If you're going to read intently over my shoulder, please make sure to brush your teeth first.'

Fizz said something so mean in reply that he was not only very lucky no one else was around to hear it, but that it was also quite untranslatable.

Trying to ignore the fact that her closest friend was also her rudest one, Jewel read on.

ATLAS LIBRARIUM
FOLIO

These words were inscribed on a scroll, bordered by a frame of small squares, etched into the leather cover. In each one, there was a picture – a butterfly, a bear, or a tree. There were some figures that looked to Jewel almost like robots, which made no sense on something this old. She decided they must be old-fashioned gods she had never heard of.

On the very first page there was an engraving of a man with sharp eyes and an even sharper beard, wearing a ruff. Scrolls were piled up on shelves behind him, and he rested one hand on a pile of books.

'William Shakespeare, I presume,' she muttered. 'It normally is.'

But then she read the inscription underneath.

NICHOLAS CROWNE NATUS WINCHESTER VI
NON. OCTOBRIS ANNO MDXLVI,
DENATUS IV NON. DECEMBRIS ANNO MDCVIII

Fizz made a sound that sounded like a strangulated 'To be or not to be' and collapsed dramatically on Jewel's shoulder with a flourish. Jewel smiled, and claw by claw, carefully retrieved him, enjoying his shivering warmth in her cupped hands while she pondered the inscription.

The capital letters, she knew, were like the ones the BBC put at the end of TV programmes to say when they were made, in Latin. So they were dates, but perhaps older than any BBC programme. And then, suddenly, she knew the answer.

They were Roman numerals, each one representing a different value.

M equalled 1000

DC, 600

D, 500

X, 10

L, 50

V, 5

18

and I equalled 1.

That made the first date 1546, and the second 1608.

All very interesting, but how on earth did she suddenly know that?

'I haven't ever studied Latin, Fizz,' she said, 'but I understand these letters. I didn't know before I opened the book, and now I do. Maybe I am a nerd, after all?'

Fizz suggested that not only was she a nerd, but the very worst kind who liked to show off. At least, that was what it sounded like.

As for the rest, Jewel had heard of Winchester, and knew it was a town in the south – but Nicholas Crowne? She had never heard of him, and shrugged, turning the crudely cut page.

She drew her school blazer in tight around her. The shop seemed to be growing colder. On the next page was another elaborately engraved panel, supported by writhing sea serpents with dog-like faces.

Jewel paused and touched her cheek. That was odd. Had something dripped on her? She glanced up at the ceiling of the shop, but only saw the dangling light and cracked plaster beyond.

'This is all very illogical,' she said to her hamster. 'Do

you think I should keep on reading, or stop?'

Fizz bounced up and down in her hand.

'Very well,' she said, 'but don't come running to me if something else weird happens.'

Slowly, she turned another page. From either corner of this panel, what looked like fat baby angels with short wings, blew gusts of wind from long thin trumpets.

The wind felt real, on her hands. That was impossible!

Fizz started in alarm, shivering at the cold draught.

Jewel held him tight. 'There's no need to be alarmed,' she said. 'I've got you.' But who was holding *her* tight? Who would tell *her* not to be scared?

Jewel stood up and walked back through the shelves to the shop door. It was as shut as she had left it. She opened it a crack, just to check, but no gale howled in. Outside in the damp, shining street beyond, traffic came and went as it had before. A couple walked past under an umbrella, gossiping quietly to each other. In the distance she heard a police car racing somewhere. Frowning, she shut the door again, let the bell tinkle and returned to her spot on the floor between the shelves, looking at the atlas that still lay there.

There was the same page, the same angels and their trumpets, and—

'Oh!'

There it was again. A sharp, cold gust of air right in her face. She felt it ruffle her hair. 'There must be a draught coming from somewhere. That's the only logical answer.'

A draught that had sent Fizz cowering behind her neck.

Trying to remain calm, she traced her finger over the top of the next page, which featured all the stars, moons and signs of the zodiac. Far below the stars, dolphins with spiky fins and giant lips leaped in and out of curling waves across the bottom of the page, and as they did, a splash of water sprayed over Jewel's hands.

She stared in disbelief.

They were dripping. It made no sense at all. For there was no water on the floor and, looking at the book, it remained completely dry, inside and out. Nothing dripped from the lamp above.

Yet her hands were soaking. She sniffed them. They smelled of salt and the sea. Fizz ran down her arm and sniffed them too, wrinkling his little nose and scratching the top of his head in confusion.

'Ceilings do not drip seawater. It's impossible,' declared Jewel. 'So I must be hallucinating.' She turned the page quickly, as if that would stop whatever was happening from happening.

Folio was not anywhere Jewel recognised either from school or from her mother's many home geography lessons. There was a land called 'The Reads', full of woods and rivers, and more drawings of little characters, some of which she recognised from all the stories and fairy tales that Patricia read to her every night. A little fairy on a butterfly. Which story was he from again?

Patricia would have known. She liked old books like this. In fact, Jewel would go so far as to say that 'liked' was a major understatement. Her mum was *addicted* to old books. Their house was full of the things. Not just on shelves or bedside tables, as in normal people's houses, but piled in toppling stacks on each step of the stairs, scattered around the sofa in chaotic islands, haphazardly surfaced with Post-its and coffee rings.

Some Patricia read cover to cover, but impatiently, as if she was in a crazy hurry, for reasons only she could see. Others she just flicked through, her nose in the air, twitching with increasing irritation before setting them aside with a sigh. A few she would hold up and shake, and occasionally a few loose pages would flutter down to the floor, now and then accompanied by a lost train ticket from another decade. Then she would flop the book down in despair and never look at it again.

It was as if her mother was searching for something, but she never said what. Jewel knew that Patricia desperately missed her younger sister, Evelyn, who had gone missing before she was born. In fact, 'missed' didn't begin to cover it. The aunt she had never met seemed to haunt her every moment, dominating every conversation, until Jewel felt there was surely nothing new to say on the subject – yet somehow there always was. But whilst she was no expert on missing person enquiries, Jewel was puzzled as to how looking in second-hand books might help.

They were all the same kind of books: either fairy tales, or books on science and the future, some of which made Jewel's eyes glaze over to even look at.

More than once Jewel had asked, 'What are you looking for?'

Her mother would shrug, chewing a biro, and discard yet another book on to the lopsided pile beside her.

'The way back.' But she never said to where.

Jewel was disturbed from this train of thought by Fizz trying to bite her finger, which she knew from experience was hamster for 'Get on with it.'

'If you insist,' said Jewel, 'but if I have any more hallucinations about draughts or drips, I am holding you directly responsible.'

Fizz puffed up his chest and glowered, giving off a low hum of rage.

Jewel screwed up her eyes, pursed her lips and glowered back.

Fizz wilted, and Jewel turned the page. 'Thank you, challenge accepted.'

Here was a map of a huge city, with thick arteries of streets running up and down, and so many buildings packed in between. It didn't look like any city she knew. There were huge pyramids, twisting helixes rather than skyscrapers, even some flying cars . . .

'The City of the Unreads,' Jewel read. She fancied that the noise of her own city outside suddenly sounded much louder, and shivered, despite feeling a strange blast of hot air on her face from somewhere, which she tried to ignore. 'Now, why does that name sound familiar?'

The next spread was covered by miniature line drawings of trees, plants and streams, jumbled and crowded on top of one another, right to the edge of the paper.

Even the scroll announcing the name of this sprawling forest was entangled with creepers, but not so much that Jewel couldn't read the name. 'The Idea Jungle.'

'Fizz, I'm beginning to suspect that this map must be of a fictional or imaginary land,' said Jewel.

Fizz gave a snort which effectively translated as 'You think?'

As if by answer, a green shoot bearing two small leaves inexplicably rose from the spine of the book, like a miniature beanstalk.

'Oh no you don't!' cried Jewel. 'No more impossibility. That's it!'

She tried to slam the book shut.

But she couldn't. She tried again. The book wasn't that heavy. Yet something was holding the covers down, like they were chained to the floor.

Then the green shoot was joined by another. And another, and another, until it looked more like a planted furrow than the paper valley of an open book. Creepers crept out from beneath the cover at an alarming rate, spreading their suckers over the pages.

Jewel sprang back in fear. Except she couldn't, because something was grabbing at her hands.

One of the creepers had flicked itself around her wrists, joined by more creepers, binding them tight.

More and more vines, spilling out of the book, spread over the shop floor, coiling themselves around her legs, her waist, pulling her towards the book.

'Fizz! Run!' Jewel managed to cry, and then the plant

plunged into her mouth, silencing her.

In less than a second another furled out and wrapped itself around Fizz, who was trying to make an ill-judged escape by nibbling a tunnel through *Collected Shipping Forecasts 1956–1958*.

Jewel's arms flailed, reaching for anything to hold on to as she got pulled further and further into the book, but only hit the hanging lamp, which swung like an erratic pendulum, until its light fell uselessly on another deserted corner of the bookcase.

But the light also cast shadows.

Wriggling, spidery shadows, of tendon-like lines of vegetation multiplying at unnatural speed as they wrapped themselves around, consumed and pulled their victims inexorably towards the one place they didn't want to go.

Outside, in the storm-streaked afternoon, Jewel's pursuers ran wearily past one last time, exhausted, soaked, and furious about their vanished quarry.

'Where'd she go?'

'She can't just have gone!'

But she had.

CHAPTER 3

The Idea Jungle

Meanwhile, Jewel was struggling and didn't stop until she realised that she was no longer in a bookshop, and almost certainly no longer in Newcastle.

She couldn't even be sure that she was still on earth.

Spitting out a large vine leaf, she unwrapped a creeper from around her head. Sweat ran freely down her temples, her neck and back. Wherever she was, it was swelteringly hot.

She blinked sweat out of her eyes, trying to focus.

There was a loud squawking above her head and she started, but it was only Fizz, unfurling down a creeper like a circus aerial artist, before landing with an angry squeak at her feet. The hamster dusted himself down.

'Well that was the trip of a lifetime,' said Fizz. 'And by

trip of a lifetime, I mean a never-ending nightmare I still can't wake up from.'

'Indeed,' said Jewel, still wondering at the clouds of greenery about her head. Then she glanced sharply down. 'Fizz. Did you just say something?'

'Say something? I shall do more than say something! The next time I visit that bookshop, I shall be complaining in the strongest possible terms, and by complain I mean shut the shop down and have the entire workforce incarcerated for life.'

Jewel realised her jaw was on the floor and tried to pick it up.

Oblivious, her now-talking hamster continued. 'The big question is, how much of this jungle floor is edible?' Fizz marched up and down the leaf-covered path, nibbling large bites out of every single one. 'Too bitter . . . Too sweet . . . Blows my head off . . . How long has this been lying here, for crying out loud? Are they *trying* to give me food poisoning?'

Jewel took a deep breath. *There is a logical explanation to all of this*, she told herself firmly. There always was. It must be an extended hallucination. Or a super-realistic dream. Perhaps she had fallen asleep in the bookshop. There was no need to panic. Instead, she should follow a calm, considered sequence of thoughts, constantly evaluating the best next course of action, and never giving into impulse. This was what all children her age would do, she was sure of it.

She disentangled herself from the creepers wrapped messily about her legs. It felt as if she had been caught in a net. Rubbing her eyes, for the first time, she properly studied the place the book had dragged her to.

'You suddenly have a lot to say for yourself, Fizz. Can you tell me where we are?'

The ground beneath her feet was mossy and spongy, dusted with layers of leaves – glossy heart-shaped spades, curling copper palms closing in on themselves – with desiccated, gossamer-thin leaf skeletons underneath.

'Well call me Sherlock Holmes and stick a pipe in my mouth,' said her hamster, gesturing to the greenery all around them, 'but would you sue me if I said a *jungle?*'

'I can confirm that I would not take legal action against you on that basis,' said Jewel, smiling despite herself.

At first sight, it was, indeed – a jungle. Looking up from the ground, it was almost as if they had landed in a corridor. A corridor of the deepest, darkest, most impenetrable green, that stretched on for miles in either direction. With a familiar sinking in her heart, despite Fizz chattering away furiously about hamster rights and pet travel insurance, Jewel felt completely alone again.

A minute ago, she had felt calm and logical, convinced she could find her way out of this. But now she was gripped by a wave of emotion that swept away all sense and reason. A book had kidnapped her and Fizz. It was impossible – yet here they were.

There was no Patricia, no teachers, no other people even, no one to turn to for help or advice. One voice in her head told her to be calm, another told her to run.

'Stop it!' she said to herself. 'I need to focus.'

She tried to concentrate on what she could see directly in front of her, rather than worrying about what she couldn't. Shrubs fought for space with lank curtains of creepers, while ferns of every size gracefully draped themselves where they could. Bestriding them all, giant trees stretched up towards a brief white square of sky that seemed not just out of reach, but so far away as to be almost an illusion.

This jungle was also not just one of plants and vegetation, as the picture in the atlas had suggested.

'Look, Fizz,' she said. 'What's that glowing over there?'

The greenery was festooned with light bulbs, bright and blinking. Every branch of every tree, every tip of every bush, dangled with a glowing light. And the bulbs were not uniform, like a row of lights in a classroom, but of many different sizes, shapes and colours.

'A party!' hissed Fizz. 'In a jungle! Is nothing sacred any more?'

The lights did indeed look like the decorations at a wedding Patricia had taken her to in a park last year, strung from trees around a little bandstand.

'Aren't they pretty!' she had said. Then they had held hands under the different-coloured lights shining through the leaves, and danced around to songs played by a jazz trio as the evening light slowly faded. She had felt happy, safe and loved.

But right now she felt anything but happy and safe. A jolt of nausea – part excitement, part fear – shook her, as she realised that these bulbs were not festooned or hung, or even wired in.

'Fizz,' she said slowly. 'Are those bulbs . . . *growing* out of that branch?'

'Plants grow,' said Fizz. 'Children grow, unfortunately. But bulbs? Give me a break.'

He was right. Bulbs didn't grow. Glass wasn't a living material. But then hamsters didn't normally talk either. And in this jungle both those things seemed possible. The bulbs sprouted from branch ends and drooped in clusters

31

from leaves. In fact, as Jewel stared hard at the bulb above her head, she saw what looked like a shimmering raindrop slide off a bud next to it.

Except it didn't slide off.

The raindrop swelled and bloomed into another bulb. As she gazed in wonder, she could see that although they burned with illumination, these growing bulbs were not like household bulbs in any way. Behind the glass, there was no filament or coil. This new young one, just above her, now filled with clouds of shifting gas that billowed impatiently in their balloon prison, as if they yearned to escape. Craning her head to stare at it, Jewel caught glimpses of something else in the glass.

They were hard to describe.

Neither quite picture or photograph, they were more than just images. A castle on a cliff, a woman's face and a shooting star exploding across the night sky . . . Each bulb had different things swirling inside the gas, or at least, fragments of things which flew around at such speed she thought the glass might shatter.

It excited and disturbed her in equal measure, like so much of this experience.

'I think we should stand back,' she warned Fizz. 'Those lights do not look safe.'

'Couldn't agree more,' said Fizz. 'A complete and total waste of public money. A scandal!'

Everything inside the bulbs was incomplete. Bricks rather than finished buildings, half-painted pictures, seeds waiting to grow and even embryos waiting to be born.

'What do you think they are, Reader Jewel?' said a voice.

Startled, Jewel looked around. The voice was rich and yet gentle at the same time, and seemed to come from everywhere.

'Who said that?'

As if in reply, there was a riffling noise, like someone thumbing through the pages of a book. The tall jungle trees that surrounded them parted as easily as those same pages, revealing at first a glimpse of nothing, a darkness beyond – and then a figure appeared, wreathed in light.

This light was so intense, radiating out from behind and within, that Jewel had to shield her eyes. This *had* to be a hallucination, yet Fizz darted behind her legs with terror, as if it was real. Through the dazzling glare, Jewel could just make out the features of a face – eyes, nose and mouth, and enough to know that whoever this was, they were kind. They glowed with a fiery radiance that came from inside.

Treading so softly that they left no mark on the leaves,

the figure stepped towards them. Jewel could just make out the outline of a cape and elegantly slippered feet. Every single flower, plant and bush leaned after the figure, drawn by the light. The stranger stretched out a hand to one of the shimmering, whirling bulbs, and examined it fondly for a moment.

'I am what Patricia and her brothers, and . . . her sister spent so much time searching in vain for.' The shining face turned back towards her. 'And yet I freely present myself to you now. Do you not consider that peculiar?'

'Peculiar?' snorted Fizz. 'You're glowing, you appeared from nowhere, and you're dressed like Sir Walter Raleigh in the middle of a tropical jungle. You give peculiar people a bad name.'

Jewel tried to ignore her hamster. 'Are you even a real person? Do I know you from somewhere?'

'You will,' said the stranger. 'For you are brought here for a reason. Look around you child, and tell me what you see. Where are we?'

And somehow, the gentleness of the voice, the softness of the light, these things calmed her troubled mind in an instant. She understood exactly where they were. The map, the name of this place. 'The Idea Jungle? But it was only a picture in a book.'

'You are surprised this is a real place?'

'It can't be a real place. Folio, the Land of the Reads, the Idea Jungle – my mother is a geography professor and I can tell you that none of these places exist on earth.'

'Your certainty is admirable, Reader Jewel.'

'This is only a dream! I don't understand how opening a book—'

'Could transport you to another world? The world of the imagination?' The figure smiled, and the flowers of the jungle seemed to turn their heads towards him. 'Then you have much to learn about how books work, Reader Jewel.' He stooped down and picked up the leather-bound atlas which now lay at her feet, covered in creeper strands, and slipped it into the folds of his robe. 'This belongs to my library . . . it has served its purpose – for now.'

Fizz whispered in her ear. 'Don't say anything. Pretend you can't hear me. But I think our caped wonder might be the man pictured at the front of the book.'

Of course! Nicholas Crowne! Jewel was beginning to understand. A librarian, apparently. At least, she presumed so, if he had a library. This reassured her, as in her experience, librarians were trustworthy and kind.

'Those bulbs, they're ideas, aren't they? That's what this jungle grows.' Then she frowned for a moment. 'But I thought ideas came from the imagination.'

'You did not think wrong,' said the stranger. 'Watch.'

Cupping his hands to his face, he made a strange kind of humming noise, the sound amplified a thousand-fold.

The noise startled Fizz, who toppled back off Jewel's shoulder.

'Wait! What are you doing?' she cried out, but it was too late.

For in reply to the stranger's call, the bulbs started to make a noise too. They didn't just distantly buzz, like faulty ones at home did, they hummed. The humming, which began as a low drone, began to rise into a kind of chorus, the like of which Jewel had never heard. A shrieking cacophony filled the air. She shrunk back, fearing again that the bulbs were about to explode and shatter her with glass. Fizz clung to her ankle in terror.

'Do not be afraid, Reader Jewel and Hamster Fizz,' said the Librarian. 'Listen. My inspirators approach.'

Over the humming came the sound of gentle wings. Wings, it turned out, that were the size of saucers, as a gigantic and very beautiful butterfly softly landed on the nearest bulb. The inspirator's wings were striped, like a tiger's, and when they caught the light, they burned with an inner fire. With great care, the butterfly injected its extra-long proboscis into the bulb of smoking, swirling ideas, and began to feed, until the glass was quite empty. Then, with a toss of its head, it flew off towards the sky.

'Has it eaten the idea?' said Jewel.

'Now there's a thought,' said Fizz, licking his lips hungrily. 'I could eat a whole lot of ideas right now. With extra sauce and some notions on the side.'

'Just watch, and then still watch,' said the Librarian.

The first inspirator was followed by more. A great, glittering host of beautiful insects, their wings quivering with delight as they alighted on the bulbs and began to drain them of their vital, swirling cargo. Jewel now could no longer contain herself and was lost in wonder, pointing and marvelling at all the different sizes, colours and patterns of the inspirator butterflies.

There were so many, and the light shining through their translucent wings painted a stained-glass rainbow on the ground. As the creatures hoovered up the ideas, either they or the bulbs released a gentle fragrance. It reminded her of mango, and peach, and ginger, and yet none of those quite described just how sweet or sharp it was.

Then, with a flurry, the inspirators departed as quickly as they arrived, floating off towards the hole of sky in the jungle ceiling, looking more and more to her like coloured lanterns as they disappeared with their precious cargo. She found herself straining after the vanishing cloud of colour and light.

'Only the foolish follow butterflies,' said the Librarian, and he took a step towards them. His voice was sterner than before. 'Especially inspirators. But all Readers are foolish to a degree. Your aunt Evelyn was. She had a chance to enter my library and learn. This she did, with her siblings, through a magic door between our worlds. They used what they learned to bring peace to Folio . . . and then, she did something no Reader should ever do.'

He looked away for a moment, cradling a large rose in his hand, sniffing the scent.

'What . . . was that?' whispered Jewel, hardly daring to ask.

The Librarian's voice was like thunder, and as he spoke, the jungle darkened. He crushed the rose in his hand, the shredded petals fluttering to the ground.

'She came back!'

The Magician Project – Extract 34
KV 1/1634-8)
Letter, Evelyn Hastings to Professor
Diana Kelly

58 Colville House, Waterloo Estate, London E2
17th February 1946

Dear Professor,

I am writing to say how sorry we all are that you
have gone to prison.

I promise that we didn't put the blame on you.

We are all right. Larry is obsessed by unicorns.
He can't stop drawing them. They all involve
Roderick, and some of them are very funny! Simon
is doing miles better. His teachers say they
don't recognise him when it comes to reading.
Father and Mother are so proud!

Patricia and I spend as much of our free time as
we can in the local library. I know that it wasn't

founded by Nicholas Crowne and isn't in Barfield, but we still keep hoping...Patricia has become mad keen on maps. She's trying to find out if 'you know where' is a real place.

We hope you are well. Are we allowed to visit and bring you cake?

Just one more question. What happened last summer? Really, though, what happened? What did you do to us?

Yours sincerely,

Evelyn Hastings

END SECURITY FILE

CHAPTER 4

Jewel is Given a Task

The Librarian's face, which had been a vision of warmth and light, sharpened into meaner features: a widow's peak, narrow eyes and a pointed beard.

Suddenly he didn't seem so friendly any more. He seemed cruel and dark and dangerous. Jewel couldn't meet his eyes, and looked at the ground.

There was Fizz, holding up a large leaf, on which he had written crudely in mud:

YOU DISTRACT HIM WHILE I RUN AWAY

Jewel had a feeling that it should be the other way around, but it didn't matter.

She was scared, but she wasn't ready to run away. Not yet.

'Is it so bad to want to come back to somewhere you liked?' she asked the Librarian.

'Not if you want to control it!' he roared. 'This is my world! I created it! It was I alone who found the way for our kind to access the world of the imagination. I created it as my legacy to all humans, but that was not enough for your aunt. Evelyn found a way back when she should not have. She tried to take control for her own ends, and instead . . .'

He gave a deep sigh that blew through every tree in the jungle, making them shudder. And, as if he had blown it into her mind, the familiar memory resurfaced.

A smell of roasted coffee, cigarette smoke and supper cooking in the kitchen. Her mother on the phone as she stirred a pot. The same conversation, the one she had overheard so many times, that never seemed to have an ending.

'But Simon, why won't you listen to me . . . I know all this . . . I don't want to give up! She is our sister, and I use the word *is* with deliberate emphasis . . . Please! It's so unlike you of all people to give up . . .'

Evie. Again, and again, the subject that never went away, and never got resolved. Patricia's sister, whom she

42

had never met, who had disappeared all those years ago and who her adoptive mother could never let go. The older Patricia got, the more haunted and obsessed she seemed to be.

Was this place, this strange world of Folio, where Patricia was also looking for the way back to? All Jewel knew was that her aunt had mysteriously disappeared before she was born. Although her mother never tired of wanting her younger sister back, or trying to find out what had happened to her, she was reluctant to discuss exact details of her disappearance.

Whenever Jewel asked, Patricia gave the same answer.

'I keep telling you, I don't know where or how! I only know that she is my sister, and I know, I feel it in my blood, she is still alive! In this world or . . . Come on, finish your cereal, otherwise we'll be late for school. Again.'

Now the mystery was part-solved.

'Evie,' she breathed. She was here, in Folio. Aunt Evie, the missing sister who her mother yearned for more than life itself. 'What did she do? Why did she return?'

'Let me show you.'

The Librarian stretched out his hand and made a gesture, like turning a page. Only the corner he turned was made of air, and the world of the jungle was just a sheet of

43

fabric, which he pulled up and stepped through as easily as through an open door. It was not clear what lay beyond. Half in, half out, he turned, beckoning her to follow.

'Well, Reader Jewel?' he growled. 'Do you want to find out what your aunt Evelyn did?'

'I think I've seen this movie,' whispered Fizz in her ear. 'And by movie, I mean the kind you watch from behind the sofa, through your hands, and then don't sleep for the rest of the year.'

Jewel took Fizz in her hands. 'Aunt Evie's disappearance has haunted Patricia for my entire life. So, don't you think—'

'We should get ourselves both killed? And on an empty stomach? Time out for me!' said Fizz, making a 'T' sign with his paws.

'Are you Jewel Hastings, the kin of Evelyn Hastings?' roared the Librarian.

She was, in a way. But was that enough? Perhaps Fizz was right. In the science experiments Jewel enjoyed doing at school, she was learning to make careful observations, record the evidence, and reach a logical decision based on the facts available.

But how did you make a decision without any evidence?

'Yes. But she's only my aunt and she disappeared before I was born. We're not even related. I was adopted, you see.'

'And are you a Reader? The fifth to ever enter Folio? Did you answer my call and open my book?'

'Yes, but I was only hiding from some bullies.'

'Well then! Your obligation is clear, and you have accepted the quest.'

A flush of panic rose in Jewel's chest, her throat tight. 'Wait! I haven't accepted anything. You never said anything about a quest. I'm a schoolgirl from Newcastle, not Indiana Jones!'

'You think you are scared now, but that is nothing as to what you must face. Come!'

He clicked his fingers, rendering Jewel and Fizz powerless to resist his summons, and by some force that felt at once both magical and dangerous, they flew through the rent in the jungle wall and into the void. She had no control over the situation at all. It was terrifying. It was wondrous.

Then they were in the sky. It was like flying and falling at the same time.

Beneath their feet were rippling circles of pleated white cloud, that vanished as they drew closer, pierced by the

Librarian's slippered foot, his robes of fur and silk billowing in Jewel's face. Pushing them away, she saw beneath the cloud, a desert which undulated in endless, empty dunes in every direction.

'How much further?' Jewel asked the Librarian, but the wind blew her words away.

Just as she began to worry her feet would never touch solid ground again, rising from the edge of the desert in the approaching dusk, she saw some towers. Unearthly, unreal, and yet there they were.

These were not rectangular skyscrapers such as she had seen in photos of Hong Kong or New York. Instead, these towers were shaped like the crescent of the moon, or the helix of a molecule – they seemed to waft and float like a stream of bubbles. Every single one was ablaze with light, and not just the white or orange city glow she was used to, but more colours than she knew how to name.

They were so strange and yet so familiar. Jewel had seen them somewhere before though . . . on a map, in a magic atlas she was beginning to wish she had never laid eyes on.

She closed her eyes as the strange towers grew closer, bracing for impact, and heard Fizz yelling something in her ear about airline refunds, then a blast of air propelled them forwards. They tumbled, clouds and land and sky revolving around them in dizzying flashes, until with a jolt, they felt firm ground beneath their feet once more.

The Librarian stood before them, as calm as if he had just stepped inside from a garden.

Fizz shook himself back into normality. 'Let me be very clear,' he said. 'The second we return to civilisation I will be sending a polite note to your immediate supervisor, and by polite note, I mean a full-scale military assault.'

Jewel brushed herself down. 'Fizz,' she said firmly. 'Don't you think it might be polite for us to find out what the quest is first? Even if we haven't technically accepted it yet?' she added, pointedly.

Fizz sniffed haughtily and rolled a side-eye at her.

Jewel rubbed her eyes free of grit. The city wasn't anything like Newcastle, the only city she had ever known, the city she had lived in all her life. There didn't appear to be any normal buildings, in shapes she was familiar with. She missed the dramatic steel half-moon of the Tyne Bridge hanging over the deep dark river of her home city. The solid, rectangular floodlit expanse of St James' Park football stadium. The thin, graceful stone column of the Monument. The only thing that seemed to be the same was the sharp spring air. The two worlds did, at least, appear to share seasons.

Yet, as Jewel gazed around at the neon lights, the swooping rooflines and curving walls, the impossibly smooth walkways, she felt a pang of recognition of something else deep in her gut. She just didn't know what.

'You want to go on this adventure, then?' said Fizz.

'I want to go home. But I don't think we have much of a choice.'

'And you think I'm going to come with you?'

'I can't do it alone.'

'Well that is the worst idea ever since someone said, "I know what hamsters want more than anything else, a wheel that never moves anywhere!"'

'Fizz, you may be able to talk here. But you are still my pet. You're coming, and that's final.'

Her hamster grumbled and chewed at some seeds from the jungle floor that he had stored in his cheek pouches, and at last gave out a deep sigh of acceptance.

'I want it noted that I am accompanying you under duress.'

'Noted.'

'Then perhaps you could begin by telling me where in the world we are now?'

'I think it must be the City of the Unreads,' said Jewel, remembering the atlas. She wondered if the Unreads were any friendlier than they sounded.

The light began to swell again around the Librarian's evanescent form, a candle flaring in the night. His voice softened, and as he spoke, he gazed beyond Jewel and Fizz, his eyes fixed on a distant point. For a split second, Jewel considered trying to run away as Fizz suggested, while the Librarian seemed distracted. But where would she run to?

'Look around you at this beautiful world of the imagination, Folio. Home to every story ever told in the Land of the Reads, and to every fact here in the City of the Unreads. It was once a chaos, to which I tried to bring some order. The inhabitants called me the Librarian, people in my own time thought me a . . . magician. I thought myself all powerful in this world, which I was not. There were consequences . . . a brutal war between Reads and Unreads, which your mother Patricia and her siblings resolved with deep wisdom. A great evil was defeated . . . for a time.' He sighed. 'However, even wise people can be foolish. Evelyn wanted to make your world a better place. But that proved . . . not as easy as she thought, so she came back here instead.'

The Librarian wandered for a moment across the vast concrete plaza they stood in. He appeared to sit down on a curved bench of shining steel, which ran the length of the square, yet in fact only hovered just above it. He ran his hand approvingly over the polished metal.

'Your aunt returned to Folio with good intentions. Equality! Progress! Yet in her impatience for change, she gave into the same temptation as I once did, all those years ago. She turned to magic . . . a magic that once unleashed, she struggled to control.'

He tapped the bench with his finger, and the entire length of solid steel fissured, before collapsing in a silent pile of dust. The magician's words were also like a blow. Jewel found herself strangely calm again. Why was she so calm one moment, and terrified the next? Sometimes it was as though there were two forces pulling at her in opposite directions.

'What has she unleashed?'

'You will find out. But it can do much worse than this.'

His glowing form began to fade into the night.

'What it's got to do with me?'

'As your mother and aunt knew all too well, Readers are the only true protectors of Folio. Only child Readers are meant to enter this world. Now you have, you find us once more in peril. Your aunt has released a dark magic which puts all of Folio at risk.'

Jewel looked at the empty city around her, which had

seemed so glamorous and exciting at first, but now in the gathering twilight, looked vast and empty and alien. It looked like just the kind of place for dark magic. But how could she do anything about stopping that? She ran away from children who called her names. She didn't even know who her real parents were. And she did seem to be different – the way she thought, the things she knew. Who was she even?

'I think you've made a big mistake. I've had no lessons on quests or missions. I can't do much, in fact, apart from angry hamster wrangling.' She found she was rubbing her hands together. 'So perhaps I should go home now. My mother will be worried.'

'Is that truly what concerns you?'

Jewel nodded, suddenly unable to speak. The thought of Patricia being all alone, miles away with no idea where she was, brought tears to her eyes. She would be frantic. And nothing she could do or say from this world would reassure her.

'I see your fears, child, but trust me, Patricia has no need of assistance.' The Librarian faded back into sight for one last second. 'It is your help I need now, and time is not on our side.'

'Please . . . will you come with me . . . and help me?'

51

'I will always be with you.'

'That's not quite the same thing!'

Inch by inch he began to disappear.

'Could you at least give me some instructions, even just a clue . . .'

His body vanished from view, only his face, which he turned upon her, remaining, his ancient eyes and mouth imploring. There were just eyes and lips left now, in a sphere of fire. They gave Jewel the biggest, warmest smile yet. The smile seemed to stretch right past his cheeks and off his face, and float into the sky. It drew her in, friendly and kind, and it made her feel safe in this strange world, if only for a moment. She reached out to touch it and the smile vanished too, like a bubble popping.

'Save your aunt Evie!'

'From what?'

'Herself!'

'Why should I do that?'

'Because only then will you discover who you truly are.'

His voice echoed around Jewel and Fizz, and then that too was gone.

CHAPTER 5

At the Unicorn

Fizz shook a tiny paw at the moon and the clouds floating by.

'Oh nice, very nice trick, Mr Magician. Tell me,' he yelled at the empty night sky, 'are you available for children's parties? Because, if so, REMIND ME NOT TO BOOK YOU!'

'Please stay calm, Fizz,' snapped Jewel, when what she meant was, *calm down Jewel*. Panic was rising within her like a dark tide.

They truly were all alone now in this alien world.

She drew steady breaths and tried to stem the confusing thoughts by focusing on what she could see, rather than what she feared.

From where she stood, the city appeared free of straight

lines, yet her surroundings felt ordered and spacious. The avenue they stood in was eerily calm, but at the same time a hum of purpose and activity murmured away underneath the surface, like a well-oiled engine. Above, the sky was as full of futuristic objects as the cityscape below. Several black orbs were dotted about, seemingly suspended of their own accord, slowly rotating and catching the light as they did so.

Beneath these floating spheres, flying cars glided about their business. They didn't rumble like real cars, but elegantly soared with rainbow-coloured wings. Somewhere deep inside her these magical machines lit a flame that may have been small and wavering, but would not go out. A flame of recognition. Whoever had designed and built this city, with its space-age architecture and futuristic transportation, was someone she wanted to meet.

She knew – she just *knew* – that she was like them.

'It's like being in a wonderful dream, Fizz, isn't it?'

'Watch out!' he cried, and they both suddenly had to leap to the side as a crowd approached, marching down the smooth, curving road – more like a flattened helter-skelter than any type of street she recognised – on which they stood.

The oncomers streamed past their hiding place under a

plastic purple tree at the side of the road. None of them said
''Scuse me pet' to each other like people did at home, but
they didn't shove either – like those in crowds sometimes
did on the Metro on match day – but glided silently along.

That wasn't the weirdest thing though.

The weirdest thing was that they were all silver. Women,
men, children, a city of silver robots. There was not one
human to be seen.

'No silver hamsters, I notice,' fumed Fizz. 'Hamsterist!'
he hissed at the machines as they slid wordlessly past.

'They aren't completely silver, either,' noticed Jewel.

Firstly, their silver skin was covered with tattoos, in
long lines all over their body. As they strode past, she saw
that in fact the tattoos were moving, streams of jumping
numbers.

More perplexing still, around every robot's wrist was
a large shiny black disc which pulsed with a dull green
glow, like a big digital watch. Occasionally they would
glance at their watch, and some would hold it in front of
their eyes, staring at it as they walked, which meant they
occasionally bumped into or knocked each other, and
yet no one seemed to mind or think this was odd. Some
appeared to be even pointing their watches at others, as if
they were taking a photo or filming. A few seemed to be

receiving instructions from their devices, and kept glancing at their watches before walking faster, and then faster, and faster still. All the robots' eyes glowed with the same dull green as their watches.

'Hello!' she called out as the machines tramped past. And 'Excuse me!' and 'Where am I?' but none of them stopped, or even replied, or even looked at her.

'Rude,' muttered Fizz, shaking a paw from her shoulder. 'Someone ought to teach you machines some manners, and when I say teach, I mean recycle you into tin cans!' He whispered in her ear, 'OK, we tried, mission over, let's go home.'

'But we can't. The Librarian brought me here to save Evie. I feel like I made a promise.'

'Sure, and every day I promise you that I won't poop on your bedroom carpet if you let me out for a run around, and—'

'Every day you poop on my bedroom carpet.'

'Yet you still love me! And feed me, more importantly.'

'It's not the same thing, Fizz. Evie is my aunt! She's been missing for years. We could save her!'

'Or we could leave now, and be back home just in time for *The A-Team*.' He gave a big smile of stained and crooked teeth. 'It's up to you!'

'How would we even get home though?'

The crowd of robots was growing larger and larger, filling the entire avenue. She tried to walk away from them but there were too many. Every step she took, she got pushed back, until the crowd was in danger of crushing her and Fizz. More and more robots piled down the avenue, closing them in on all sides.

Then there was a fluttering in the open sky, far above their heads. A noise Jewel was sure she had heard only recently, but where? Looking up she saw, flapping brightly in the sky like a welcome flag, the most unlikely thing to see in a city of neon and steel, seemingly miles from where she had first seen one in the Idea Jungle.

An inspirator. It was perhaps the most magnificent one she had seen yet, with tiger stripes so golden and so vivid she almost expected to hear it roar. But even more astonishing still, this butterfly had a rider – a tiny fairy.

As this pair descended towards them, the robot crowd silently moved away.

'Oh great, a small person. A hamster's worst nightmare,' moaned Fizz. 'If he tries to ride me he's going to get the shock of his life, and by shock, I mean—'

'Wait. I think I've seen him somewhere before.'

Was it from the map? Or in one of the many fairy-tale

books Patricia had bought, borrowed, read and thrown aside?

This fairy was wearing an acorn on his little head, and his clothes were so wispy they might as well have been made from cobwebs. It was clear he was looking for something too, peering over the butterfly, swooping down into the crowd and then out again. Then he caught sight of her.

'Aha! Here you are at last, my dear, and not a moment too late!'

'I could say the same to you,' said Jewel, looking around at the space the robots had now cleared for the new arrivals, glad she could breathe once more. She felt a rustle on her hand and looked down to see the tiger-striped inspirator gently perched there, with her tiny fairy rider doffing his acorn cap. His pale face was angular and sharp, his features worn.

'Sir Tom Thumb at your service. Fairy Knight at Arms, representing the Land of the Reads at the Folio Federation. This fine creature is Majesty, Queen of the Inspirators, a fairy steed since time began. And you, my friends, are both most welcome to Folio,' said Thumb in his cracked voice. 'Now, Jewel Hastings, tell me, how is dear Reader Patricia?'

'She's fine. I think. Kind of. Wait – how does *everyone* know my name, and my mum?'

The word 'mum' caught in her throat, as it always did.

She loved Patricia and she knew Patricia loved her. But who was her real mum? In many ways, the answer was the same. Patricia, of course, who had raised her, given her so much. Lying under the surface of her thoughts all the time, though, like some sinister dark shape moving through the depths, was the great unanswered question of her existence.

Who was Jewel Hastings and where did she really come from?

But Thumb wasn't listening.

'And what of the other Readers? Simon and Larry? The last I saw of them they were determined to find our lost Librarian, the magical creator of us all. But I suspect they never did. They could no more find him than we could find any remains of the monstrous King of the Never Reads or his magic mirror.'

'Who was the King of the Never Reads?'

'Now there's a tale. But quick march, or we'll be late.'

'What does it take for a hamster to catch a break in this town?' said Fizz. 'Kidnapped by a book, flung through the air by a wizard, now frogmarched by a fairy. Would it be too much to ask for, I don't know, a NICE WARM CAGE and maybe just a tiny ball of fluff?'

'For once, I agree with my hamster,' said Jewel, folding her arms.

'I take it all back immediately!' said Fizz.

'Why should we follow a fairy on a butterfly? Where's the logic in that?'

Thumb narrowed his eyes and stared at her suspiciously. 'Logic? You talk in a very strange way for a little girl, Reader Jewel.'

She swallowed, suddenly as self-conscious in front of him as she was with her classmates.

'Well . . . at least tell us who these robots are?'

Thumb shrugged. 'The Unreads! All the facts, data and information in the world, walking around in perfect, gleaming, technological form. Whereas I am a—'

'Read? A story character?' Fizz yawned. 'Old news, my friend. The glowing dude in the cape already told us.'

'And these are my people,' said Thumb sternly.

He pointed ahead of them, where another strange helter-skelter road joined their one. Jewel could see a very different-looking crowd approaching along it.

There was not much gleaming silver here, apart from the armour worn by dashing knights on horses. Instead, here were the inhabitants of the Land of Reads, including some of the witches, dwarves, and giants Jewel had seen depicted in the Librarian's atlas.

There were so many people, monsters and animals surging forward in the dusk, that it was hard to make them all out. But one thing was for sure. The Land of Reads did contain every story character ever read.

For alongside long-standing residents the Pied Piper of Hamelin (with a long line of rats squeaking behind him), the tiny inhabitants of Gulliver's Lilliput, and all the animals from *The Jungle Book*, she also spied Willy Wonka in his colourful tail suit, Dennis the Menace, and Gandalf from *Lord of the Rings* with his great staff – not to mention thousands and thousands from tales all over the world that Jewel could not yet begin to name.

Every fact in the world ever discovered, every story ever told . . . they were all here, Jewel realised. Every single one of them wearing the same glowing green disc around their wrists. Not just robots, but school children, lions and wizards. Even the Famous Five were wearing them – Timmy the dog had one around his collar. Every single inhabitant of this magical land.

Majesty surged ahead, Thumb urging Jewel and Fizz to follow, and having nowhere else to go, they did, weaving through the endless tide of Unreads and Reads to keep up with them.

The road twisted and turned until finally it arrived at a vast structure, radiating coloured lights in every spectrum of the rainbow.

'Fizz, is that a giant unicorn's head?' said Jewel.

'Nothing about this ridiculous country surprises me any more,' said Fizz.

But it did Jewel. From the great head, a tall golden unicorn horn pierced the night sky, an oversized flagpole from which hung a sail of billowing silk, bearing a single, ornate letter 'F' for Folio.

Two silent concrete unicorn eyes gazed down over the crowd gathering beneath them, with the inscrutable, implacable coldness of a sphinx. Except that it also appeared to be wearing a pair of pince-nez glasses constructed from light steel. The coloured lights strobed the air from the tufts of the carved unicorn mane, and its vast open mouth housed a majestic staircase, which led up to an imposing and grandly lit balcony that stood quite empty, apart from a line of robots standing guard.

'What are they guarding?' asked Jewel, as Thumb brought Majesty to a halt at the back of a huge crowd which filled the concrete square in front of the unicorn.

There was a hush of reverential expectation.

'Our most sacred and precious monument, built in memory of a great war hero, Roderick the Unicorn. But we just know it now as the Unicorn, and those are the most highly trained robot soldiers in the kingdom. The Unicorn Guard. Or, as we call them, Screamers.'

'Why?' said Jewel, bracing herself as more and more Unreads and Reads buffeted her from every side.

'Let's hope you never have to find out,' said Thumb grimly, wheeling round on Majesty.

Jewel could see that they looked almost beetle-like, their bodies a series of armoured and polished shells linked together. Unlike the Unread citizens, they did not look remotely human. They had no eyes, no mouth, no face, only an impenetrable polished dome for a head. And most striking of all, the robots of the Unicorn Guard were not silver, but shining green all over, the same emerald colour as the light glowing from the discs that everyone seemed to have fixed around their wrists. Everyone apart from Thumb, Jewel noticed.

'Excuse me,' she said, 'but why haven't you—'

'Quiet,' said Thumb. 'I think it's about to start.' But he didn't say what *it* was.

The entire crowd was transfixed by the Unicorn,

watching the spectacle on their green discs or holding the discs up in the air to film it or take a photo. A barrage of electronic drums pulsed from deep inside, making the whole unicorn head shudder. High-pitched digital trumpets wailed from concealed speakers. Finally, the whole wall behind the balcony slid upward, revealing a glowing internal chamber.

In time to the drums, the lasers sparring in a frenzy above their heads, figures marched out. Jewel scanned the crowd in desperation, hoping to catch sight of just one other human being, anyone to make her feel less alone. The calm Jewel was fading, the emotional one returning.

Then, she caught sight of her. Just a flash of a child's face, as young as her own.

It wasn't the silver of an Unread, the green dome of a Unicorn Guard or any story character that she recognised.

It was a face made entirely out of copper.

The Magician Project - MAY 1948, INF /166)
Newspaper article on release of
Professor Diana Kelly

DAILY HERALD
FRIDAY MAY 7TH 1948
'MAGICIAN PROJECT' PROFESSOR RELEASED
By our Crime Reporter

Professor Diana Kelly, the Ministry of War
scientist notorious for her part in the
'Magician Project' affair at Barfield Hall,
was today released from HMP Shepton Mallet
after serving her full sentence of two years
for offences against the Official Secrets
Act. Speaking briefly to reporters outside,
Professor Kelly, 67, maintained her innocence.

'No one was harmed by my experiment,' she
said. 'The only harm that has been done has
been by the British government to an

experiment that had the potential to transform human lives for the better. But that is in the past and today I announce my decision to retire and return to civilian life.'

'What will you do instead?' called out one reporter, to which Professor Kelly replied: 'What do you think? Read books, mainly,' before climbing into a waiting car.

The so-called Magician Project was a controversial and unauthorised experiment into psychological warfare techniques led by Professor Kelly just after the end of the war. Full details of the affair are still classified, but there was widespread outrage at the involvement of children, all from one family.

The children involved were unavailable for comment, but when reached by telephone, their father Frank Hastings said, 'It's not right what happened, not right at all. The law is the law, but if that Professor was to show her face around here - well, I wouldn't like to say now, would I?'

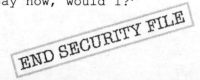

END SECURITY FILE

CHAPTER 6

Exit the Empress

This copper girl was another robot, as machine-made and expressionless as the others. And yet. There was something in her eyes, Jewel was sure of it. They locked on to her own. She saw the moulded copper curls on this other girl's head, the permanently pursed mouth, and behind her electronic glare, something that made her move her own lips in a wordless 'Hello.'

If the copper girl acknowledged her she couldn't tell, because just then some silver Unreads blocked her view trying to get closer to the Unicorn, and the copper face disappeared. Jewel reluctantly returned her gaze to the great balcony at the top of the monument steps as the drums and trumpets built to their frenetic climax.

Spotlights swung their aim on to the balcony as more

polished Unicorn Guards strode into view, escorting three bears. They looked like a family: a mother bear and a father bear, with a younger baby bear. For some reason the old fairy tale of Goldilocks popped into Jewel's head, but she didn't remember the bears in that story wearing crowns, or velvet capes, or clasping jewelled sceptres.

One of the guards placed a tall microphone on a stand in front of the bears, while another dragged two modern, angular chairs on to the balcony. The two older bears, who looked very grey around the muzzle, collapsed on to these metal thrones, while the younger one strutted forward to the microphone in his tiny gold circlet and velvet finery.

'There are eight known species of bear,' muttered Jewel, 'but I am not aware of one noted for royal dress and speaking into microphones.'

Eight known species of bear? It was like the Latin numerals. How did she know all these things?

'What did you say?' replied Thumb, giving her a curious look.

'I mean, don't tell me the bear's going to talk as well,' said Jewel with a laugh and a blush, automatically trying to cover up her own unexpected cleverness, just as she did at home.

'Of course Baby Bear can talk. He's the Vice Regent,

the Empress of Folio's official deputy,' said Thumb, and there was a cold edge of suspicion to his voice. Jewel was glad to have an excuse to look away, as Baby Bear began to address the crowd.

'Citizens of Folio!' he declared gruffly, raising one paw. 'Remember what you know!'

The entire crowd copied his gesture, and repeated mechanically after him, 'Remember what you know!' Even Thumb did the same, also doffing his cap just as he had when they first met. Copying him this time, Jewel raised her hand tentatively and repeated his words.

Baby Bear growled, a deep bearish rumble from the pit of his stomach. Even though he was far above her head on a balcony, Jewel still flinched as his claws glinted in the light.

'All hail her Highness! Empress Evelyn the First, Reader and Supreme Ruler of Folio: Unreads, Reads and all the Lands in between!'

The electronic drums fired up again, and a figure escorted by yet more guards emerged from the glowing chamber behind the Vice Regent, who retreated, bowing, to the side of the stage.

This time the new arrival was beamed not just on to the many glowing wristwatches around Jewel, but projected into the sky above all their heads as a giant, rotating hologram.

A woman, spinning slowly in the dark night air, ablaze with light. Her figure was bent and huddled, almost swallowed up by her own rippling robes of grey. Then she lifted her head, and the cameras could focus in on her face. She looked pale and tired, her features almost obscured by the blinding lights. But there was no doubt in Jewel's mind. It was a face she had seen before, in so many of Patricia's dog-eared photos and albums.

Evie.

Her missing aunt. The woman she had been dragged into Folio to save. There she was, on every screen, in the sky, and standing for real, right in front of her.

'The Librarian was right. She's alive!' she said to herself, torn between fear and adoration as her aunt began to speak.

'Remember what you know,' began the Empress.

Her voice sounded like treacle slowly running through gravel. It was tired, but strong. With the same four identical words, she projected more grace, power and wisdom than Baby Bear ever could. So why was every word like a knife being twisted in Jewel's gut?

The crowd murmured their customary response but this time, Jewel couldn't manage it. Her throat was

70

suddenly choked, her eyes brimming as she watched this woman high on a distant platform.

That was upsetting enough. What was more upsetting was that she had no idea why. Brushing away the tears, she tried to focus.

Far above them, Evelyn continued her speech.

'My beloved citizens of Folio. I have been back in this beautiful world for over twelve long, happy years. I was a Reader whom you accepted with love as your ruler, even though the Librarian had forbidden my return.'

Applause rippled through the crowd, but Jewel found herself thinking of the glowing magician who had sent them spinning through the air, the thunder that crossed his face when he spoke of Evie's transgression. What could he possibly be expecting Jewel to save her from?

'It has been twelve incredible years. More and more stories have joined the Reads, and more and more Unread facts have now been discovered. You have welcomed each other with kindness and respect. And, of course, we have discovered Folio's greatest invention yet.'

She held aloft her wrist, which Jewel now saw, also had a glowing green disc affixed to it.

Everyone else in the crowd, Reads and Unreads alike, held up their wrists, their discs glinting in the floodlit glare of the Unicorn.

'For the first time since the Librarian assembled you all here in this world of the imagination, I found a way to organise you. Every single inhabitant of Folio connected by the same network, a system of boundless imagination and comprehensive information, that we could all access, be we a humble fictional talking bear or a fact-powered robot, just through this one device on our wrists.'

'If only that bear who introduced her was humble,' said Tom Thumb, shaking his head sadly.

'The Stampstone! An invention so simple, yet so powerful, it would change all our lives,' said Evelyn, her voice cracking with pride. Everyone's stampstones now pulsed with the green glow, the same light that shone from the Unicorn Guard. Perhaps it was a trick of the light, but her aunt's eyes almost seemed to have a luminous green halo as well, impossible though that was.

'We were more connected. We could find out anything we wanted in seconds. Where does this character live? What will the weather be tomorrow? How long would it take to read all the books in the world? This simple stone, worn on our wrists, could tell us everything. We worked harder, we lived faster, and we were never, ever bored. It is the single proudest discovery of my reign. We have done so much together. But I am from another world, and now I must announce that . . . it is my time to return.'

For a moment her words hung in the air like an echo, before the reverent hush exploded into a babble of protestations and cries, from Reads and Unreads alike.

'No! Don't leave! You can't!'

'Who will lead us?'

'Why are you going?'

Evelyn calmed them with her hands, then reached inside her robe and pulled out a small book bound in black leather, the yellowing pages visibly rough and warped.

She brandished the book high above her head.

'In a moment, I shall return to my own time, the way I came here – the only way to come here – through a book. The very same story that brought me back all those years ago.'

Jewel and Fizz looked at each other with a glance of recognition.

'But first, let me explain why I am leaving you now,' continued Evelyn into the microphone. She lowered her head for a moment, and Jewel felt again a strange stirring in her heart as she saw her aunt's thin grey hair, glaring in the harsh spotlight. She seemed much older than Patricia, even though she was her younger sister. Jewel wondered if something had happened here to age her so much. Was it the worries of being a ruler?

Evelyn looked up again, her face wracked with pain.

'I am returning because I am dying. An incurable disease that is wasting me from the inside. Even the finest medical minds of the Unreads cannot defeat it. But perhaps my own world will have the answers. Even if they do not, at least I may pass my final days with my own family of Readers who I have missed for so long. A family that does not just include brothers and sisters, but . . .'

She paused as there was a disturbance in the crowd, robots and story characters alike chattering with alarm, raising arms and pointing fingers, some even running. The chatter turned to cries and shouts.

'I do not like this,' said Thumb, gripping Majesty's reins tightly.

Then Jewel saw why. Something was blocking the hologram of Evelyn in the night sky.

In fact, not just blocking it, but ripping a hole through the simulated image of her face like a dark claw. The giant claw kept on coming, smashing through lasers, now heading for the crest of the Unicorn . . .

Not a claw, but some winged beast. A beast of such size that it seemed to obliterate light. Every beam or ray that touched it disappeared, as if they were shining into a black hole. Only by the void it left in the illuminated sky could Jewel just make out the curl of a tail, the length of neck.

Like a monstrous bat, the creature swooped down on to the huge stone balcony, sending the Bears fleeing inside the monument. Now in the harsh glare of the floodlit stage, the full horror of the intruder was revealed.

Heavy scaled legs of deep ocean green, pawing the floor with clawed feet. A long swollen body, dwarfing every other living thing in sight. Great hooked wings now folded up to their half size. And at the end of a coiling, searching neck, the head of a monster that Jewel did not believe existed outside her books.

Two eyes that burned with the crackling, blinding light of life. The unmistakeable cold thin smile of an ancient reptile, which opened into terrifying, dripping jaws, showing startling white teeth and a pink tongue against the forest floor skin.

Dragon skin.

The Unicorn Guard raised their arms, and their hands began to glow.

A laser ray, which seemed to be full of numbers like the lights pulsing over the Unreads' bodies, fired out, but the monster replied with jets of flame, reducing the robots to piles of melted metal in seconds. Panic swept through the crowd, some of whom tried to run, while others stood, as if hypnotised, capturing the dragon on their stampstones. A blizzard of tiny light flashes swept across the arena like a host of fireflies as they took photos or videos.

Some brave story characters – a woodcutter, a princess and some toy soldiers – somehow clambered up on to the concrete balcony, but met the same fate as the robots, the microphone cruelly broadcasting every last scream of agony and crackle of charred bone as the dragon incinerated them too.

All this, too, recorded on the stones of those watching.

Evelyn, however, stood stoic and upright. Dignified, calm and untouched by fire.

She opened her book.

But now Jewel could see the dragon was not alone. The folded wings slowly lowered to the ground, like doors . . . And sitting astride its ridged back was a tall knight in armour. The green of his armour matched that of his mount.

'No!' cried Evie to the knight. 'You promised!'

She looked down at the book and a golden light seemed to curl off the pages, like steam. The crowd pushed and shoved around Jewel, more and more trying to run. Thumb yelled in her ear, but she was quite immovable. Her gaze was fixed on the woman beginning to disintegrate in the curling clouds of light as the book drew Evelyn back to the world of Readers. The human world they shared.

Then the green knight dismounted, as cool and steady as if he – for Jewel assumed it was a he – was all alone on a quiet summer afternoon. With one heavily armoured arm, he flung Evie's book into the air, where a blast of dragon flame caught it, sending a shower of useless, smouldering wet ash to the floor.

With the other, he grabbed Evelyn, who struggled and kicked and bit – and dragged her on to the dragon behind him, oblivious to the drifting clouds of smoke and fire from the burning robot guards that now filled the stage. As the great wings extended for flight and the monster prepared to take to the sky, thundering down the long balcony in fast, deliberate steps, a voice rang out.

'No! You can't take her! It's wrong! She's dying. Let her go home!'

Jewel was shocked. Someone was shouting, challenging the intruders. The crowds parted as this person ran forward towards the balcony, robots looking as startled as robots can. Who would dare to risk their life in such a way?

Then she looked down, and realised it was her. She

was waving her hands and shouting, her face tight and hot. They couldn't take her aunt! She was dying. She had to go home. The Librarian said Jewel had to save Evie, so she would—

'Come back!' hissed Thumb. 'Don't let them see you!' But he was too late.

Silver robots and fairy-tale characters had already made way for her, quickly spreading out in a circle as she approached the monument.

Where was the Librarian now? He said he would always be there.

But there was nothing, just Unicorn Guards approaching, a bear yelling in the distance, and the glittering pale belly of the beast swooping into the sky.

Jewel felt a lightness behind the eyes that spread to the rest of her head, and remembered that she hadn't eaten anything since breakfast. Nausea billowed through her, a sickness consuming all her senses, her centre of gravity shifted . . .

The world swam in a blur of glowing light and steel, and as she fell, staggering into an outstretched pair of metal arms, the last thing she saw was what looked like a distant emerald star, streaking across the night sky.

NATIONAL SECURITY ARCHIVES

SECURITY FILE

The Magician Project – Extract 34 (KV 1/1634-8)
Letter, Evelyn Hastings to Professor Diana Kelly

58 Colville House, Waterloo Estate, London E2

4th May 1946

Dear Professor,

Why won't you reply to my letters?

I know it is the right address. Do you have any idea how difficult it was to find it out? I had to go to the library – the real one, near our house – to look up the newspapers about your trial and find out what prison they sent you to.

They shouldn't have sent you to prison. What you did was amazing. I don't know how you did it. I just know I want to go back.

They made us sign the Official Secrets Act. We aren't allowed to talk about it to anyone. We aren't even meant to discuss it amongst ourselves,

79

although of course we do, when Mother and Father aren't around. But I dream every night of Folio. I remember everything that happened as if it was yesterday. The magic library door, entering the City of the Unreads, the city that glowed with light. A glass queen called Jana, the tiny flying Fairy Thumb, a man inside a tree, the darkness that nearly swallowed us all.

I see them in my dreams, Professor. But what happened - it wasn't a dream, it wasn't a film, it HAPPENED.

A robot nearly dissolved my foot with numbers. I saw a blank page rise out of the earth and crush our enemies. I realise now that ideas are real, as hard as stone. That stories are living things. They live in a world that truly exists.

I can't forget them. There is so much I still need to learn. I could be someone there. They offered to make me Ruler. I could change things.

Help me to go back to Folio.

Yours sincerely,

Evelyn Hastings

CHAPTER 7

Pandora

When Jewel finally awoke, roused by the golden slice of sunlight draped over her bed, she first hoped that she was in her own bedroom, safely back at home.

A huge pile of teddies and other soft toys tucked to one side of the candlewick bedspread, the crumpled A-ha poster above her headboard, and, plastering the adjoining wall, family photos, from her first faltering steps, to the seaside holiday in Scotland last year dressed in a bright-orange lifejacket on a boat, licking an ice cream.

But the toys, poster and photos were nowhere to be seen. She looked in vain for her pride and joy, the combined radio *and* double cassette player, in glossy red plastic, covered in fruity scratch-and-sniff stickers, next to a wobbly stack of mix tapes ... How she wanted to be

somewhere familiar, somewhere she recognised!

She wasn't. The bed, which was much larger and more comfortable than her own, looked on to a cool, airy room, with light flooding in from a sloping glass roof.

On the wall opposite, a large TV – as flat as a mirror, unlike the bulky box they sat in front of at home – broadcast pictures of waterfalls flowing into forest pools, the sun setting over a tropical coastline, and hot-air balloons drifting over lush plains. The room hummed with gentle background noise, presumably from concealed speakers, which was either running water or a soft breeze – she couldn't quite be sure.

The events of the previous day felt like a bad dream, or a film featuring someone else, someone who only looked like her. And now here she was, in a room so strange and futuristic, that—

'What's up?' A bedraggled Fizz poked his head up above the sheets before snuffling out over the immaculate bed cover. 'I have a feeling we aren't in Kansas any more, and by Kansas I mean suburban Newcastle in 1984.'

'I do feel like I'm in a dream,' agreed Jewel. But then she looked down at her wrists and saw the marks where the creepers from the book had bound them, and remembered the glowing figure in the jungle, the inspirators, the Unreads, her aunt on the giant Unicorn's head swept away by a knight on a dragon, and a wave of nauseous panic curdled her thinking. It was like everything she believed to be true had come adrift, untethered from its mooring.

She scooped up Fizz. 'Please tell me this *is* a dream. Because if all this is real, then I'm not sure I even know who I am any more.'

Fizz stared at her with his beady blackcurrant eyes.

'Kid, you've never known who you are.'

Jewel looked away, biting her lip.

He sighed. 'I'll tell you what you need. What we both need. A slap-up breakfast.' Before she could argue back, he wriggled out of her hands on to the floor, marching about and bellowing. 'Hello, room service? Is anyone there? I could eat a prize-winning carrot and all its nearest relatives. And get my owner a bowl of Frosties before she goes out of her tiny mind!'

Jewel had been so exhausted she could only half remember arriving in the room, escorted by the green robots of the Unicorn Guard, Fizz tucked safely into her blazer pocket. Had she been offered anything to eat or drink? Maybe a glass of water. In the end she had just collapsed on this big comfortable bed as soon as the guards shut the door on them both, falling into the longest, deepest sleep.

A sleep filled with actual dreams, haunting her mind over and over, with the same distant hologram figure twisting in space for eternity. The missing sister who had made her mother so unhappy for her whole life.

And she sat bolt upright in bed.

Her roiling mind steadied itself.

She was not confused and disorientated. She was focused, purposeful. A logical plan now presented itself, the only way forward. Evie was alive. She had seen for herself – all too briefly. Whatever had happened to her last night, whoever had taken her, Jewel would fulfil the Librarian's command. She would save the aunt she never knew. She was going to bring her back home. The doctors there would make her better. They had to, because last night, Jewel thought that she saw something else. She thought that—

One of the walls slid noiselessly open, and standing there was the copper girl she had spotted in the crowd the night before. Jewel started and pulled the duvet up under her chin as the only means of defence available. Fizz adopted his hardest stare.

Jewel was about to challenge the robot on why she was

in this room, what was going on, who was in charge . . . when she saw what the copper girl was carrying.

A tray on which lay one large carrot and the biggest bowl of Frosties Jewel had ever seen, sparkling with sugar and drenched in milk.

'Hey,' said the copper girl, in a clear and cheerful voice, 'I am Pandora, and here is the breakfast you just requested.'

'Thank you, Pandora,' said Jewel. She took the bowl of Frosties carefully, so she didn't spill any, and then devoured it faster than she had ever eaten a bowl of cereal before. She was so hungry she almost forgot to tell Pandora her name. 'I'm sorry, I'm—'

'Reader Jewel Hastings,' said the girl, 'and welcome to the Imperial Palace! My name is Pandora and I am your assigned assistant for the duration of your stay.'

'And what about hamsters?' said Fizz, already demolishing his carrot in a frenzy. 'Do we get an assigned assistant? Because I like how this is going so far.'

'Hamsters are rodents,' said Pandora. 'Traditionally kept in cages, I cannot identify a need for a personal assistant at this time.'

'A pleasure to meet you too!' He huddled up to Jewel in a sulk.

'But Fizz is my best friend, Pandora,' said Jewel.

'I am your assigned assistant and the best friend you can ever have!' said Pandora. She pointed to a large black disc in the centre of her chest that pulsed quietly with green light. 'Like all Unreads, with this latest generation built-in stampstone I can answer any question, direct you to any location, and perform a range of useful tasks. But I am also different. The more time I spend with you, Jewel Hastings, the better I will get to know you. I will know you better than yourself!'

Jewel folded her arms and narrowed her eyes. 'We'll see about that.'

'Yeah, we will,' said Fizz, who briefly stood on his rear legs, folding his tiny front legs and narrowing his eyes as best he could.

Jewel smiled. But was her closest companion really a hamster? And did that matter? Would a robot girl be any stranger? One thing was for sure. Friendship had to be earned. 'In that case, can you please tell me where I am and what is going on?'

'Fetching your location! One moment while I search the Stampstone . . .' The robot thought and then said, 'Your location is . . . the Guest Suite, part of the Imperial Folio Palace complex, City of the Unreads. This location is

86

currently closed to the public. Would you like to know when this location is most popular?'

'No!' said Jewel, 'I want to know *why* I'm here.'

'Searching . . . The meaning of existence has long been debated by philosophers and scientists,' said Pandora. 'But it's a big question with no definite answer. Now, would you like a bath?'

Jewel was about to reply when she felt a very sharp nip on her arm. Trying to smile through the pain, she said, 'Thanks Pandora. Can you just give us a minute or two?'

'My pleasure!' said Pandora, bowing. Pressing a button, she opened a panel in the wall, revealing a polished and tiled bathroom beyond. She stepped inside. 'Have a great minute, up to a maximum of two! If you ever need any help, just say, 'Pandora! Help!' and I will endeavour to fulfil your request.'

The door hissed shut behind her, a lock clicking into place.

'I don't trust her an inch,' said Fizz, at the same time as Jewel said, 'I can't believe how human she sounded!'

They both stared at each other, and Jewel suddenly felt ashamed. Fizz was right. Pandora hadn't explained why they were locked in this room, or who had put them there. But then again . . .

'I know you're suspicious, Fizz,' she said gently. 'But to be fair, back home, you are suspicious of the postman and he's never done you any actual harm.'

'Yet!' snarled Fizz.

'Until she arrived,' said Jewel carefully, 'we were trapped in this room. She arrived with food and is offering us a bath. I'm not saying we should trust her, but she might be able to help us get out of here. And every second we delay, and stay here, Evie is . . . well, I'd rather not think about it.'

Fizz thought for a moment, and then grumpily agreed. 'Be warned, though. I shall be watching her every move. And yours.'

'It looks like you both need to freshen up,' said Pandora, emerging from a now steaming bathroom to hand Jewel a fluffy bathrobe and Fizz a small flannel. She had run a hot, deep bath for them, overflowing with bubbles.

'Smells like, you mean,' said Fizz, as Jewel sank beneath the surface. Fizz perched on the rim of the tub, doing a kind of acrobatic dance with a miniature loofah.

Once she was clean and dried, Jewel changed into the simple but comfortable tunic that Pandora had left folded outside the door.

It was nice to be fed, to be clean, but as the comfort of the hot water wore off, the nightmare of the previous night once more clouded her mind.

'Pandora. Last night, the Empress was kidnapped at the Unicorn. Why isn't anyone doing anything? Why are you giving us cereal and baths as if nothing is wrong?' The robot just blinked at her. 'You must have seen it too! Don't you believe me?

'Would you like me to play the song, *Believe in Me*?'

'No! I want you to help us get out of here. Please.'

Pandora hovered, staring at her, the black stampstone in her chest pulsing quietly. The robot looked like a girl, her voice was full of animation, the expression moulded on to her copper face was not unfriendly. The voice sounded a lot like a real human being, even if not always making as much sense. And every time she moved or her skin shone, she looked like a robot. But still . . . she made Jewel feel something.

Like they had a connection.

Was she being daft? Could a machine ever be like a person?

Jewel's experience of robots and speaking machines was so far limited to the droids in the *Star Wars* movies, a speak-your-weight machine in the Eldon Square Shopping

Centre, and a school trip around the Nissan car plant in Sunderland where automated arms sprayed electric-blue paint over car doors.

But Pandora could not have been more different. Perhaps she could trust her.

'Pandora,' Jewel began carefully. 'I know everyone – including you – is just trying to keep us safe. But I have been brought to Folio for one reason only. To rescue my aunt – your Empress. Why wouldn't you want to help someone save your ruler?' She folded her arms, satisfied by what she regarded as her unimpeachable logic.

Pandora hummed for a moment, lights pulsing. Then her stampstone glowed an ominous red and her voice darkened. 'You were an unidentified intruder in the city at the time of the Empress's abduction and are now a suspect in custody.'

The smooth floor might as well have opened up beneath Jewel.

'A suspect! But she's my aunt! I was trying to help her! I'm not a dragon!'

'Well,' said Fizz. 'That is a matter of opinion.'

'You have to let us go! Immediately.'

'It sounds like you are trying to contravene the laws of the Federation of Folio. Would you like me to report you to the authorities? Or terminate you now?'

Pandora raised her left hand, which began to pulse with light, and Jewel remembered the laser rays the Unicorn Guard had fired at the dragon.

'No!' she said, shrinking back. She thought Pandora had been smiling, but she now realised her face had no expression. It was just copper metal and light and data. The only expression was in her voice, and was that even real?

'Please – I'm sorry . . .'

'Reporting you now. You are being confined on the orders of the Vice Regent himself. Please do not be alarmed.'

The robot walked swiftly to the sliding doors.

'Wait!' said Jewel. 'Please! I thought you were going to be my friend!'

The robot turned and looked at her long and hard. For a flickering second, Jewel swore she saw the same look in Pandora's eyes that she had given her in the crowd the night before. A look that wasn't robotic or cold or unfriendly. Then it vanished, as quickly as it had come. She tapped a key pad on the wall, and the door slid open.

Jewel remembered something the robot had said earlier.

'Pandora! Help!'

But her assistant was blank.

'I am unable to fulfil that command at the present time.'

Then without another word, she left, and the door slammed shut again, leaving the girl and her hamster all alone in their prison.

CHAPTER 8

Screamers and Spriggans

The Imperial Palace Guest Suite was completely sealed. Yes, the bed was comfortable, the air conditioning set to the perfect temperature, and they were accompanied by a ready supply of Frosties and carrots, but there was no getting away from it. Fizz and Jewel were prisoners.

All day long she banged and hollered at the doors with no response. She slapped at the window but the building was so far away from any others that no one heard. And even if they had looked up from their stampstones for a moment, what would the Unreads have done? She was their prisoner, after all.

'Why won't they listen to me? Don't they understand? We need to rescue Evie . . .' Her voice drifted away to a miserable murmur.

'I'm not an expert, but perhaps it's because you're talking to a wall?' ventured Fizz. 'Maybe focus on finding a way out of here instead?'

'That is easy for you to say. Hamsters spend their lives escaping from things.' She glanced at him. 'Wait – could you not chew your way out and get help?'

'Sure,' he said. 'I'll just chew through several tonnes of solid glass, steel and stone. It might only take a thousand years, but we'll get there eventually.'

There was that queasy sense of rising panic again.

As their first evening in custody approached, Jewel wondered, would they ever escape? Jewel wasn't sure she could take another day of it, never mind a thousand years. In desperation, she explored the suite for what felt like the twentieth time. Could she somehow tip the bed up and use it to smash the window? To her relief, the bed was screwed to the floor.

There were no other loose implements anywhere – it was just a giant luxury prison cell. So she tried to logically evaluate what *was* in their room. What could she do with a pillow? Or a fluffy towel? Or the breakfast tray left on a table?

'Wait a moment,' said Jewel, looking at the empty Frosties bowl and scattered carrot peelings. 'I have an idea.'

'Excuse me while I fetch my hard hat and retreat to a safe distance,' said Fizz.

Jewel knelt and cleared the tray. It was metal with a ridged edge. She took careful aim and hurled it at the sliding door.

It bounced straight back into the room, nearly hitting her in the face.

'That was a great idea,' said Fizz, 'and when I say great, I mean the worst idea in history since you decided to hide in a spooky bookshop.'

But Jewel Hastings was not defeated so easily. She picked up the tray once more and pondered. Then she remembered the time that *they* had trapped her in the toilets. She hadn't wanted to fight – that wasn't her thing. They had mocked her, jeering her on to strike back, but she had resisted.

Then, in desperation, she had spotted the fire alarm glass, never meant to be broken except in case of an emergency. In her view, the situation had become an emergency. With a swift swing of her school bag, bulky and pointed with books as ever, the overhead sprinklers had been activated and the bullies dispersed. Or soaked, at least.

There was no fire alarm glass in here. But there was a panel of sorts. A key panel.

With Jewel deploying the tray like a battering ram, the key panel collapsed with a hiss of breaking glass and electrics after a couple of attempts. What remained of the lights behind it flashed erratically, and the door opened. And shut again. And opened.

Jewel trusted that Patricia, once she told her about this, would never again complain that the endless hours she spent playing *Donkey Kong* on her Nintendo were a waste of time.

She watched the door juddering backwards and forwards, slamming into the wall with a drunken hiss each time. She grabbed a pillow off the bed and threw it in the gap, where it was crushed, the stuffing oozing out.

Then she scooped up Fizz into her pocket. 'Are you ready to make your escape, Fizz?'

'You can't be serious,' he said, watching the heavy glass door repeatedly slam against the stone wall.

But she was. Jewel watched some more, counted, took a deep breath, and jumped . . .

Clearing the entrance in one full bound, the pair tumbled on to a paved driveway that wound its way downhill between cropped lawns and ponds. The lights and towers of the City of the Unreads beckoned beyond in the early dusk.

Down and down the hill they raced, only daring to look back once – which was when they ran straight into Tom Thumb on Majesty, her elegant head rearing in defiance.

'Reader Jewel! My dear child!' he hissed in alarm. 'What are you doing out here?'

'I'm escaping, to go and rescue my— to save the Empress Evelyn. What does it look like?'

'Escape? But we were coming to rescue you. You are in grave danger.'

'I knew it!' said Fizz from her pocket. 'I say we go back to the place where they bring you free carrots for breakfast, no questions asked.'

Jewel sighed and swept her hair back from her face. 'Yes, I deduced that when the robot told us we were criminal suspects and locked us in. And thanks, but as you can see, I don't need rescuing.'

Thumb nodded his head in admiration, but could not agree. 'You will, though, you will. On that note, may I introduce you to my two personal fairy guards, Sir Ossian and Lady Jenifer Pencarrow, and their inspirators Splendour and Worship. They are brave spriggans, and will make sure we come to no harm.'

Her eyes were now adjusting to the Unreads night – which was never wholly dark but permanently tinged with fluorescence from the glittering helixes now towering ahead of them – and Jewel realised that Thumb had not come alone. There were two other fairies with him, hovering on their own butterflies.

An ancient man and woman, as small as Thumb. The hands that held their butterfly reins were gnarled, their backs hunched and their knees knocked. Their heads seemed too big for their bodies, with pointed ears and wizened goblin-like features contorted into permanent scowls. Neither of them looked very friendly, an impression only exacerbated by their suits of chain mail which seemed to be woven out of the thinnest holly branches. The spriggans tapped their brows in fairy salute at Jewel.

''Ow do,' said Sir Ossian Pencarrow. 'Little slip of a thing, ain't she my love?'

'Such a poppet,' said Lady Jenifer. 'I could 'ave 'er for lunch!' she added with a cackle.

'Nice to meet you too,' said Jewel, wondering how on earth these tiny fairies were going to help protect her against more than a mosquito. She turned to Thumb. 'Am I really in danger?'

'See for yourself!' He gracefully steered Majesty out of the way, and marching down the avenue towards them, Jewel saw the green robot sentries who had originally escorted her to her luxury prison. Then, there had only been about five of them. Now, there were dozens, marching in lockstep, with only a glowing green line where their eyes should be.

The Unicorn Guard.

'Screamers. You must have automatically alerted them when you broke out of the Palace,' muttered Thumb in despair. 'That wretched stampstone – everybody knows everything all the time, now.'

The sentries came smartly to a halt, rank after rank, blocking any way out. There was a pause, and then they parted to admit Baby Bear, still clasping his jewelled sceptre.

He looked down his long snout at Thumb in disdain. 'Thumb. I might have known you were behind this. Once a traitor, always a traitor.'

Thumb unsheathed and shook his sword at the bear. 'You are the traitor here! Why have you taken this girl prisoner? She is a Reader, for story's sake! The niece of our beloved Empress.'

The Vice Regent scowled and looked at his stampstone.

'I only have your word for that, fairy. It says here that your friend was apprehended at the scene of the crime last night. She appeared from nowhere, just as our glorious Empress was so cruelly taken from us. When she has answered all our questions, she will be free to go. As will you.'

Thumb shook his head. 'I fear sometimes, Vice Regent, that the wretched stone on your wrist has distracted and muddled your brain. This Reader was sent by the Librarian himself to save the Empress!'

The bear scoffed, and brandished his glowing stampstone at the fairy knight. 'You really shouldn't believe everything a butterfly tells you, fairy. The Stampstone knows everything there is to know truly in Folio. It will find the Empress for us. And until we do find her, *no one* is above suspicion.'

Jewel had had enough. She had heard worse rows than this at school. Every day in fact. But normally such rude and short-tempered fights were between children. Not leaders. She calmly spoke over both.

'But I have to save Evie— the Empress. The Librarian told me to. And last night, when I saw her at the Unicorn, I realised—' Tears, unbidden, once more filled her eyes. She couldn't, or didn't dare, articulate why. 'Please. You don't understand. I have to find her.'

Baby Bear stepped forward with a glinting smile. Was it Jewel's imagination or did his eyes have the strange green glow of the Stampstone as well?

'The Empress would want me to protect you from unscrupulous and bitter fairies. You are much safer with us, little girl.'

'I bet you said the same to Goldilocks!' snarled Thumb, his pale face dark with fury.

'If only you had embraced this glorious technology, perhaps we wouldn't be in this mess!' said the bear.

'The Stampstone is taking over everything! Can't you see! Looking at it all the time, I almost think you let it make decisions for you!' exclaimed Thumb.

Jewel seized her moment. 'I'm afraid it doesn't matter what either of you say. I was brought here to save Empress Evelyn, and that is what I am going to do.'

No one had spoken to Baby Bear like this for a long time. He stared at her in total astonishment. 'But it's not up to you, Reader!'

Thumb smiled. 'Have you forgotten so soon, Bear? I cannot believe we were once on the same side. Or does the Stampstone contest that too? The library law written into our origins, the foundation of our existence?'

Baby Bear frowned for a moment.

'Readers always rule,' said Thumb.

'Which means I *will* rescue Evie,' added Jewel.

The bear looked at them both, and then burst into

laughter, doubling up and slapping his furry thighs. Eventually he stopped, gasping for breath and wiping away the tears from his eyes with a large claw.

'Oh dear,' he sighed. 'You do make me laugh sometimes.' Then his face hardened and his black lips rose to reveal his rows of very sharp teeth. 'Have you forgotten where you are? Three little fairies and a girl in the great City of the Unreads?'

He looked down at his stampstone, eyes focusing in, and tapped at it. In direct response to his commands, serried rows of Unicorn Guard stood to attention with a deafening clank. Jewel braced herself. The guards' green domed heads flashed briefly, and then they began to live up to their name. They did not raise their arms to fire a number ray this time. They screamed.

Jewel had come across the expression 'blood curdling' in books and comics before, and had always wondered what it meant. The sound emanating from these robotic insects in their green shells was like no sound on earth. High-pitched, whining, and so intense that it felt more like a wave of air pressure than just a noise.

It stirred and heated her blood into a boiling, bubbling river, burning through her veins. The screaming rippled into her ears, her brain and her chest, making her entire body vibrate. Immediately she clamped her hands to her head but it was no good, she might as well have used an umbrella against a tsunami.

Her hands came away hot and sticky.

Blood.

The shock of it made her dizzy and pale, and she fell to her knees. The more the screaming went on, the harder it became to focus. Where was Fizz? She dreaded to think what a sound wave that made her ears bleed was doing to him. But she could no longer see her hamster. Her vision was blurring, the Bear was laughing, and something was buzzing around in front of her – on a butterfly.

The thing spoke to her, but it was so hard to hear through the screaming . . .

She had to concentrate. She had to.

One of Thumb's guards. The old man. Sir Ossian. His face was pale too, and blood streaked from his goblin ears, but he was tough and old, and clinging on to his confused butterfly, circling in the air like a damaged helicopter, one of his arms hanging free.

'Here, take my hand, lassie . . .'

His words sounded distorted, a record on the wrong speed. Barely able to see, Jewel waved her hand in his direction till she folded it around a tiny, shrivelled claw.

'That's it. You're my treasure, you see. And my lady's got hers.'

Out of a half-closed eye, Jewel saw Lady Jenifer clutching hands with Thumb. What good would holding hands do against this wall of sound, destroying them from the inside?

'My lady!' called Sir Ossian.

'My lord!' replied Lady Jenifer.

'Spriggans protect their treasure. Spriggans awake!' they both called solemnly together.

Jewel cried out in surprise. To her astonishment, the tiny hand in hers was growing larger and larger. It grew and grew until the hand was in fact encircling hers. Then not just her hand, but holding Jewel herself in its rough wrinkled palm that smelt of barley and lavender. The enormous hand scooped her off the ground, lifting her high into the air, away from the noise . . .

Her head beginning to clear, she looked across at Thumb . . . Who was sitting in the palm of an equally vast Lady Jenifer. He winked at her.

The Spriggans weren't fairies at all. They were giants.

The Magician Project - Extract 38
(KV 1/16383)
Letter, Professor Diana Kelly to
Evelyn Hastings)

> Corner Cottage
>
> Dunstall
>
> Suffolk

July 16th 1953

Dear Miss Hastings,

I don't know how you found my address. I must politely ask you to desist writing to me.

It remains a matter of great regret that I was not able to speak to you further about your experience in Barfield. I fear much of what the gentlemen from the government may have told you is untrue. Of course, I long to know more about what you saw and what you discovered...but for the sake of my own career and health I am obliged to put that all behind me.

My post is opened before it arrives. They will have read your letter. They will read this. I dare not say any more. But perhaps they will not censor this, if I tell you XXXXXXXXXXXXXXXXXXXXXX XXXXXXXXX [REDACTED]

Yes, Barfield was a scientific experiment, but not of the kind described in the papers. I had your wellbeing – all of you – uppermost in my mind always. I knew there was something magical about that house from the moment I arrived, and I could see that you and Larry did too. It created a kind of atmosphere, didn't it? One all of its own.

Yet what he saw, and what you saw, despite what you may insist, took place entirely in your own minds. None of it was real. Mrs Martin and myself may have assisted your visions by XXXXXXXX XXXXXXXXXXXXX and XXXXXXXXXXXXXXXXXXXXXXXXX [REDACTED]

I fear I have already said too much.

Please do not write to me again, and please under no circumstances make any attempt to visit. The house is watched. My advice to you, my dear Evie, is to forget the whole wretched business as best you can.

Don't go back to Folio. There is no going back now. It will never be the same. Get on with your life. Be happy. *Remember what you know.*

Yours sincerely

Professor Diana Kelly (retired)

CHAPTER 9

A Council of Fairies

The giants towered above the Imperial Palace, Baby Bear now just a tiny furry blob miles below shaking a miniature fist. Robot screams wailed through the air but their power had waned; Jewel, Fizz and their rescuers were now safely elevated out of range.

From her perch in his dry palm, Jewel peered up at the oversized face of Sir Ossian. It wobbled above her on his wattled neck, like a papier-mâché model of a giant's head made for a parade. The fairy monster looked so unreal, yet blood ran through his ruddy cheeks and his bulging eyes were wet with excitement.

'Now that's the tonic,' Sir Ossian declared in a thundering voice, giving a long stretch with both his arms as he did. 'Been too small for too long, ain't we my love?'

'And no mistake!' Lady Jenifer replied. 'All cooped up I was! Shall we away then, my flower?'

'We shall, my duck. Spriggans advance!'

They began to stride through and over the City of the Unreads, as easily as if it was a toy town. The helixes and pyramids and flying cars disappeared between their legs.

Something was trying to snuggle in her tunic pocket.

'Fizz! The Screamers. I was so worried about you.'

He poked his nose out and scratched at his ears. 'Screamers? Ha! They should spend some time in a litter of twenty-five hamster pups like I did – now *that* is screaming to be scared of.' He stretched, yawning. 'Now, if this is long-haul, I'm going to try and catch forty winks before they show the movie,' said Fizz. 'Wake me up just as they're serving the cheese.'

Fizz curled up snugly in her tunic pocket, his eyes shut tight, his paws over his snout.

'Fizz?' whispered Jewel.

'What now?' he replied drowsily, turning over, trying to get comfortable.

'You may be the grumpiest and rudest hamster I know—'

'And let's be fair, that's a very short list.'

'But I'm so glad you're here. That I'm not alone.'

Fizz made a noise that sounded like he was trying not to gag, but Jewel smiled all the same. As he started to snore heavily, she peered over Sir Ossian's fingers, the night air rushing past her face, then curled up to stay warm, just like her hamster, as she looked down over the scattering Unreads and Reads.

Jewel wondered if Pandora was amongst them. It was true, she was a robot like the others. Except not completely like the others. A copper robot in a sea of silver, with advanced capabilities. Yes, she had locked them in their prison, but was that her choice or a system over which she had no control?

She had watched a movie once, *War Games*, about two teenagers who nearly started a nuclear war by playing games with the computer which controlled the American missile defence system.

Computers followed instructions, and it was not always possible to override them, once given.

'I will be your best friend,' Pandora had said.

But what did she mean precisely? Could she ever compare with Fizz, Jewel wondered.

Either way, what use was a hamster or a robot, however loyal, against the creature she had seen at the Unicorn? A dragon the size of an aeroplane, which incinerated anything

110

that dared come near it without a moment's hesitation. She shivered and nestled into the giant's hand.

Lady Jenifer drew closer to her husband as the alien lights and screams of the robot city faded into the spring night behind them. Tom Thumb bobbed into view, sitting comfortably in her palm. Majesty rested next to him, quivering patiently, alongside her fellow inspirators Splendour and Worship, who had not transformed in size, unlike their riders.

'Spriggans are ancient fairy guards,' he explained. 'Often they guard buried fairy treasure, only turning into these giant forms when disturbed by intruders. It's not something they can do very often. And inspirators can't do it at all. Although they can do many other things . . .'

'When was the last time Sir Ossian and Lady Jenifer got this big?' asked Jewel.

'Oh, probably about six hundred years ago,' said Thumb cheerily, as if he was talking about last week. 'And after this they'll need to rest for another six hundred years before they can do it again!' He glanced across at his fellow passenger fondly. 'You're worth it though, my dear.'

'A brave young Reader,' chuckled the spriggans above them, in another burst of thunder. 'Now that's proper treasure!'

Jewel wasn't sure she wanted to be anyone's treasure, but she was very glad to be far from the Screamers and their bear commander. She turned away from the fairy and rested her chin on her folded arms, gazing down at the dark woods and trees that now appeared below.

There was the black gleam of a lazily winding river, with clusters of homely roof tops and smoking chimneys – candles in windows, lanterns on hooks – gathered in the bends, and the soft broad backs of cows, grazing by hedges and fences.

Thumb drew in a deep draught of air. 'The Land of the Reads!' he sighed with delight. 'The home of story. Isn't it fine? Isn't it rare?'

'What's that though?' said Jewel in alarm, pointing to a dot in the sky beyond. As they got closer, she was relieved to see that it was not another dragon, but one of the floating spheres she had seen in the sky above the City of the Unreads. Close up, it looked like a gigantic black bowling ball suspended in the air, rotating constantly.

'Lady Jenifer!' called out Thumb. 'A little bug to your right!'

Without breaking her stride, the spriggan's other great hand reached out and grabbed the bowling ball, crushing it between finger and thumb, in a small dusty explosion of electrics, glass and metal. The ball dissolved to nothing, leaving only a dusty smear on her fingers.

'An imperial oculis – one of the Stampstone's many eyes,' explained Thumb with a grimace. 'I never agreed with the decision to let them hover over our land, but I was overruled by your aunt.'

Jewel's eyes widened. 'You know her?'

Thumb permitted himself a rueful smile. 'If I had been the first person Evie met when she first came to Folio then things might have been very different indeed. But I wasn't. And our history is . . . complicated.'

There were so many questions. Questions she had never asked Patricia because she had never wanted to encourage her mother in her obsession about finding Evie. But now, she wanted to know everything.

'What was she like? What did she do?'

Thumb chose each of his words with precision, as if he was plucking each one down off a library shelf. 'I believe that above all, your aunt wants to do good, and that she believes she is a good person. Which is why she explained to me that for the Stampstone to be truly useful for all the citizens of Folio, to truly know *everything*, then it had to see *everything* that went on in our world.'

'And what else did she tell you?'

But Thumb was no longer listening.

'Aha! Here we are at last! A place that prying eyes must never see.'

It was still the middle of the night, but by the light of the moon, over the top of the giant's hand, she could see they were approaching a small hill. A gentle mound all on its own, swelling out of a patchwork of meadows fed by a meandering millstream.

As they approached, the air grew thicker with that sweet early summer smell of fresh grass, and Jewel could hear a bird calling from a wood somewhere. It woke Fizz, who poked his head out and, for once, seemed something close to content as he took deep breaths of the balmy air.

Then all of it was suddenly much closer, as the spriggans began to shrink.

'Here we go, my lamb!' chuckled Sir Ossian.

'After you, my pet,' sang Lady Jenifer.

Down and down they went, Sir Ossian and Lady Jenifer guffawing with delight as they got smaller and smaller, until in no time at all, Jewel and Fizz were rolling out of Sir Ossian's hand.

What had moments ago seemed very far away, like a pretty picture from a dream, suddenly became a knot of very real branches and catkins as Jewel found herself entangled in an alder bush overlooking the millstream.

The three inspirators struggled to take wing as their riders once more mounted them, the spriggans bent over with exhaustion, Lady Jenifer already beginning to snore very loudly, slumped over Splendour's back.

'And here we are, brave Reader,' said Thumb, deftly whisking a powdery catkin out of Jewel's hair with his sword. 'Welcome to Fairytale Valley. The safest place in all of Folio. But we must hurry!'

But Jewel shook her head. 'Not until you tell us where and why. Every minute that goes by, Evie could be further and further away. Your Empress is dying! What part of her speech did you not understand? Or did you also miss the massive dragon which swept her away?'

'Shall I spell it out for you?' warned Fizz, rearing up on his hind legs, air boxing with his front ones. 'And by spell, I mean knock into your head letter by letter.'

Thumb softened his tone. 'I understand your concerns and, trust me, no one shares them more than I! This is why we brought you here. But, as one of my detective colleagues in the Land of the Reads is fond of saying, the game's afoot. Not all is as it seems. There is something you need to know first. Onwards, Majesty!'

Thumb flew out of the bush and up the hill, followed by

the slumbering spriggans, weaving dozily behind him on Splendour and Worship.

'Shall we make a break for it?' said Fizz, who had already rubbed mud on his face in camouflage stripes and was covered in more twigs and leaves than a member of the Territorial Army on weekend manoeuvres. 'I'm an expert on survival. I once spent a whole week locked in a pet shop on my own, living off nothing but shredded *Daily Mail* weekend supplements. I couldn't get rid of the taste for weeks.'

Jewel did not smile. There was a darkness brewing in her mind, darker than the depths of this summer night. 'Thumb's right. There's more to this than meets the eye. We follow him – for now.'

To follow the fairy was harder work than she expected. They had to push through overgrown clumps of willow, hazel and dogberry that blocked their way, Fizz deftly scampering under them.

The inspirators wove through a copse of ancient oak, Jewel wading after through ferns that curled up to her waist, Fizz devouring as many seeds and fallen fruits as he could along the way.

As the ferns grew thinner, so the slope grew steeper, until at last they emerged from the shade of the old trees on to a bare hilltop, the one Jewel had seen from her perch on Sir Ossian's hand.

Bare, apart from a clearly marked circle of toadstools. Red domes spotted with white freckles that seemed to glow in the moonlight. Mysterious tall skinny white caps on slender stems stood apart like sentry towers, and interspersed amongst them all were broad flat discs so purple that they looked black in the half light, squatting low to the ground like angry toads.

'Oh wow,' said Fizz, licking his lips. 'You never said anything about a buffet!'

'Hold back,' Jewel said, doing her best to restrain him. 'There's something strange about this place.'

It was true. There seemed to be nothing within the circle, only the darkness of the soft summer night. All the same, there was no way she or Fizz were going anywhere near those toadstools, never mind touch them.

Thumb flew Majesty right to the edge of this ring, where she hovered and he whistled.

At first there was silence.

Then came another low long whistle in reply.

'By what right do you seek to enter this enchanted ring of fairies old and true?' said a rasping voice from the darkness beyond.

'By right of oak, and ash and thorn,' said Thumb solemnly.

'And when oak and ash and thorn are gone?' asked the voice.

'I came in with oak and ash and thorn, and when they are gone, so shall I too,' said Thumb, and Jewel couldn't help noticing a quiver in his voice as he said this.

'If you be true, then let this fairy ring be on view!' called out the voice.

At this sign, a light began to glimmer in the dark circle, like a candle being lit. Then one candle became two, and then more, as the ring transformed into a shimmering haze of illumination, as bright and soft as the stars in the sky.

Thumb floated through the toadstools on Majesty, escorted by the still slumbering spriggans, and vanished, seemingly swallowed up by the darkness.

'Are we meant to follow you?'

Jewel paused on the burned grass between the toadstools, uncertain.

'Stand not alarmed,' said the voice from beyond. 'For what you see is not real, but rather, charmed.'

'I don't know if I wholly believe in fairy magic,' said Jewel. 'You can't be sure of the consequences.'

It was true, she had just been rescued by a tiny

fairy with the help of size-changing spriggans. But that didn't alter the fact that Jewel Hastings had been born in 1972. She had grown up in a world of motorways, television news and supermarkets. The whole idea of living, breathing, supernatural creatures with magical powers, even in this strange world of Folio, was somehow harder to believe than screaming robots and interconnected stampstones recording your every move.

'I'll believe in anything if they've got a nice pile of wood shavings to curl up in,' said Fizz, yawning.

'But come in do, for as you see, they believe in you!' replied the rasping voice.

A little hand plucked at Jewel's and then she felt as though she was flying through the stalks and caps of oversized fungi into the circle. Fizz followed on behind, carried by another invisible figure.

At first, the dazzling lights blinded her. Adjusting to their glare, she realised that her hand was still held by a creature no taller than her waist. Pointed ears stuck out from underneath a blue cap, which sat over a wrinkled, freckly face, brightened by sharp little eyes glittering like coins in a fountain.

'I am the oldest of the old,' he said. 'They call me Puck, and this Puck's Hill, a sacred place that is older still.'

119

He swept his hand around, trailing a shower of sparks as he did, and Jewel saw now for the first time, that the fairy ring was far from empty. For sitting around in a circle were creatures she had only ever seen – if she had seen them at all – in the pages of books or created through special effects on screen. But here they were, real and close enough to touch.

'My eyes!' said Fizz.

Ogres and giants sat alongside monstrous trolls behind an extraordinary host of goblins, imps, hobbits, leprechauns, pixies and gnomes, forming a crowd some six or seven rows deep, carefully arranged on a grassy bank.

Silently they gazed at Jewel, as if they were drinking her in.

'Why are they staring at me?' said Jewel. 'What do they want?'

Majesty deposited Thumb lightly on her shoulder. He took out his sword and pressed it into her neck, making her freeze.

'In a land of stories, that rarest of commodities.' His voice darkened. 'The truth.'

CHAPTER 10

A Dark Tale

Even though a fairy was lightly pressing a sword into her neck, even though a hamster was whispering into her ear, 'I told you, I *told* you,' even though it was deepest night and she stood quite alone facing an assembly of the most supernatural and extraordinary creatures, and even though she wanted nothing more than to curl up on the soft grass and fall into a deep, dreamless sleep, Jewel Hastings stood her ground.

She had managed to switch to the cool, logical side of her brain. She didn't know how, but she had.

Her feelings were like dozens of snakes swimming under ice, wriggling around, hissing and trapped. Taking a deep breath, she kept them tamped down.

'My mother told me never to talk to strangers,' she said,

pointing to the fairies, goblins, giants and imps. 'Especially ones looking like that.'

'Puck!' snapped Thumb. 'Explain to the girl. And hurry along, there's a good fellow. Time is not on our side.'

The older fairy, in a meticulous (but endless) series of rhymes, explained how the Fairy Council was a secret gathering of all the fairy stories in the Land of the Reads. As some of the earliest stories ever told, the Fairy Council met to discuss and protect the interests of fictional characters.

Then Puck reached under his blue cap and produced three leaves. The familiar serrated fan of the oak, some oval ash leaflets on a stem, and a prickly sprig of thorn. 'Our sacred leaves, the oak and ash and thorn. Whoever takes the leaf, takes the floor, so think before you—'

Jewel sprang into the middle of the circle, plucking the oak leaf out of Puck's wizened palm. There was a gasp of astonishment from the crowd. Puck looked up at her, his eyes wide, and every trace of his impish smile melted from view.

'This is the Fairy Council, sacred, grave and true. Reader dear – that leaf was not for you.'

Jewel shook her head, and clutched the oak leaf tight. It felt dry and sharp, yet comforting at the same time.

Fairy and elfish ears twitched in anticipation. The air grew still and heavy.

'Maybe it wasn't, but you know what? I don't care.'

'Dear Reader patient be, and please speak as if you know your prosody . . .'

'Does that mean rhyming?' said Jewel. 'Because if it does, I can't. I'm sorry. This is all very interesting, exciting even, and thank you for rescuing me, but I am so tired. And hungry. And confused. I don't know . . .' Her hands clenched in frustration as she revolved around, trying to make herself understood. Finally the words came to her. 'You asked me for the truth. Well, I swear on this leaf, on my life, this is the truth.'

She looked up.

From the greatest giant to the gnarliest gnome, they were transfixed. The summer breeze itself seemed to miraculously still, and by the pale moonlight, her audience might almost have been statues. (Apart from Fizz, who was doing his best cheerleader impression at her feet, using two dandelion heads as pom-poms.)

'The truth,' Jewel continued, 'is that I am very, very frightened. I need your help. Please. The Librarian brought me here for one reason only.'

There was a ruffle of wings and horns at this.

'To save my aunt . . . Evie . . . your Empress. But he never said anything about saving her from a dragon.' She bit her lip. 'I don't care though. I know I'm just a child, but you must believe me – I am going to save her. I can't explain how yet. I just know that I will, even if I never do anything else. I must. But I can't do it alone.' She looked imploringly around at the wide eyes of her audience. 'Please. Won't somebody help me? I'm scared. That's the truth.'

And with that her legs finally gave way and she sank to the ground, exhausted. Fizz mopped at her brow with a damp moss sponge and fed her drops of water from a swollen seed gourd.

'Ding ding!' he whispered. 'Atta girl. Round one to you, champ. Next time, go for the knockout!'

The shadow of inspirator butterfly wings fell over her shoulder, and she heard Thumb declare to the crowd. 'Reader Jewel! There is nothing braver than to admit your fear. You have shown yourself to be honest and true, and worthy of the Fairy Council.'

'Worthy of what?'

'The information we are about to reveal to you.'

He slipped off Majesty down on to the ground, peeling blades of grass off his cobweb shirt. Each one was taller than him. 'Listen. I will never forget the day when your

124

aunt returned, over a decade ago now,' he said quietly. 'She just appeared at the bottom of my tree, brandishing a book. "I'm back, Tom Thumb!" she called, slapping the trunk, so the branches shook leaves down upon her head. "I'm back! I'm back!" Straightaway I flew down on Majesty to greet her, and I will always remember the sight of that face, much older, but burning with the same passion—'

Thumb stopped suddenly, and Jewel noticed his eyes were filled with tears.

'She just looked so happy,' he said quietly. 'From that moment, everything changed. Evie had this . . . energy about her, a determination. Her only desire was to make the world a better place. She did so much good!'

There was a ripple of acknowledgement from the fairy crowd.

'She gave the Green Man protected status as a tree,' said a goblin. 'So no one could chop him down!'

Jewel didn't know who or what the Green Man was, but she liked trees and nodded in approval.

'Female Unreads were built with the same processing power as male ones. Can you believe it that they hadn't been before?' wondered a giant.

'And she gave orders for a rocket to be built to take them to the moons of Folio. No one had seen anything like it!

Fairies are one thing, but flying into space? Now that's real magic,' marvelled a little pixie.

Even ancient Puck had to smile at this.

'Your aunt believed in fairness, in equality, in progress,' continued Thumb, 'many things that were not yet achieved in her own world. We did not always agree with our robot friends over the border, nor they with us, but we were at peace, finally.'

The grey-bearded giants towering over the rest of the Fairy Council from the back row nodded sagely, rubbing their chins.

'But that bear and his robots tried to kill us!' said Jewel, struggling to understand.

'The kingdom is in uproar. Our Empress has been kidnapped! That leaves Baby Bear now in charge, as Vice Regent. He is facing huge pressure to identify a culprit and . . . he has never taken warmly to Readers, I'm afraid. You are a newcomer and stranger, and, without an obvious suspect, an easy scapegoat.'

'Come on, come on,' said Fizz, scampering a figure of eight around Jewel's feet. 'Get to the good stuff. We all know it wasn't Jewel. The big green guy and the dragon! Who sent them?'

Thumb cocked an eyebrow. 'That is the question. Or,

some might even say, *what* sent them? But thereby hangs a tale.' He looked at Jewel, and behind him Puck clicked his fingers with a little explosion of stars.

Suddenly, quite overwhelmed by the excitement and exertions of the evening, Jewel found herself gratefully accepting upturned acorn cups full of the sweetest milk she had ever tasted, and cakes of honey and saffron served on broad dock leaves by bowing elves. Then Fizz snuggled up close as, curling up in the grass, pixies made her a pillow of lavender and rosemary while gnomes gently laid a blanket of woven reeds over them both.

Then the fairy knight, settling so lightly on her drowsy shoulders, began to tell her a story, although it seemed for all the world more like a dream.

'About ten years ago, there was a routine mining excavation by Unreads right on the border of this land, on the shores of the Frozen Sea—'

'The Frozen Sea?' said Jewel.

'Folio is a land of the imagination, my dear, but it is still a land and where the land ends, there lies the Frozen Sea. A vast plain of frozen water surrounding the edges of our understanding. League after league of empty sea, yet to be colonised by either Reads or Unreads. Except it turned out that this sea is not as empty as it first appeared. For buried deep on its barren shore, the robots discovered a new kind of stone with magical powers—'

'The Stampstone!'

'The very same, and these were no fairy powers,' said Thumb, 'but a beautiful, shining black stone that could magically show words, pictures, moving images. You could speak into it and convey messages. It could even measure your heart rate if you wanted. We called it an enchanted mirror, but Evie christened it Stampstone, inspired by the library stamps you use to manage libraries in your world. There was almost something intelligent about the way it could be connected to every single computer system of the Unreads. Almost as if it wanted to be used! And it was, by everyone, wearing these discs carved from it.'

'But not you,' observed Jewel.

'We that know the magic true, have no need of devices new,' said Puck.

'Although we could recognise how the Stampstone transformed Folio,' added Thumb.

'How?' said Jewel.

The fairy shrugged. 'Everyone knew everything all the time. People didn't need to remember anything because it was always stored on the stampstone. And at first we couldn't believe how much simpler this made everything.

Food supplies ran high, the weather was good, and one page turned after another, until . . .' He buried his head in his hands. '. . . your aunt lost something.'

'What? A battle? What happened? Tell me!' Jewel had never before been gripped by a story as much as this one of her missing aunt.

'Oh my dear, Evie lost something far more precious than a battle.' His face grew as cold as the midnight around them. 'Her heart. She fell in love!'

'What? With who?'

About ten years ago, Thumb explained, he had accompanied the Empress on a scientific expedition to the Ghostly Glades, where every spook, phantom and poltergeist who was ever told in a ghost story lives.

Very little was known about this region of Folio, as the Glades are cold and hard to reach, and not often visited. Vast marshy plains of long grasses border an impenetrable network of forested swamps, where tall trees sink their tangled roots deep beneath the black water.

The Empress took some top Unread scientists in her flying car to the edge of the marshes. They landed and put the car into amphibious mode. A small outboard motor appeared at the rear, gently propelling the explorers along the winding waterways.

Unreads don't generally show fear, so they were not troubled by the rustling in the trees, the large shapes moving silently in the dark water, or the ever-lengthening shadows as they approached the Glades.

But Evie felt her skin crawl as the boat sputtered under the overhanging trees. Unfamiliar birds called out and every branch seemed alive with scuttling insects, some as large as her hand and hairier than a bear. She shuddered and tried not to look. The only other option was to look over the edge of the boat, yet she found to even contemplate what lay in those dark depths far worse a prospect.

'Yet it was in those waters, gilded with a kind of mercury by the silver evening light, that she first noticed it,' said Thumb. 'A reflection. Not of her, or her companions, but of a face in a helmet. A knight in shining armour of the deepest green, somehow greener than the grass and leaves themselves.

Evie looked up. There on the opposite bank, by a crooked mangrove, stood a knight. A pennant flapped from the peak of the helmet, but she could not make out the markings on it, only that there was a crown, indicating that the wearer was a prince.

Something passed between them, something intense and beautiful, and then the stranger swiftly turned and disappeared into the shadows.

The Empress immediately ordered her Unreads to give pursuit. They tried their best to navigate the labyrinthine channels of the swamps as swiftly as they could, but the prince had long disappeared into the night.

Eventually, after hours of fruitless searching, Evelyn returned to the Imperial Palace. She sent out search parties to find this mysterious green prince. The Glades were combed by land, air and sea. Every citizen was ordered to look in every home, but no green prince was to be found.

It was not even clear which story the knight was from. There are green princes in other stories and histories, but they either denied it was them, or falsely claimed they were.

Maps of the Glades and every inch of Folio covered her office desk, walls and floor. Artist's impressions of the prince's helmet were distributed to every citizen on their stampstones – until, unable to sleep one night, scrolling through these sketches on her own disc, Evie had a revelation.

She had not seen the prince before. But she had seen the armour.

In fact, she was staring right at it. On her wrist.

The colour was the same as the glow that now lit up her face, the helmet made of the same glassy material that nearly every citizen of Folio spent their waking hours gazing into.

The green prince was made of stampstone.

The Magician Project – Extract 38
(KV 1/1792-18)

NOTES RETRIEVED FROM THE BODY OF DIANA KELLY*

Professor Diana Kelly died on the evening of 10th November, 1953, in a car accident not far from her home in rural Suffolk. It appears she swerved to avoid another vehicle in the dark, drove into a tree and was killed instantly. The other vehicle could not be traced and police continue their enquiries. These notes were found sewn into the lining of her handbag, along with the letters from Evelyn Hastings and other documents not yet declassified for release.

To whomsoever finds these notes, please forgive their hasty and rudimentary nature but I am not at liberty to write at length or in detail.

In fact, I am not at liberty.

They let me live in this wretched cottage with

its garden of lupins and dahlias as long as I play the part of a nice old lady who has retired to the Suffolk coast, to tend these plants, go to church on a Sunday, and pleasantly pass the time of day with my neighbours.

But I am watched. There are men with five o'clock shadows parked in a Morris Minor across the way, pretending to read the *Daily Mirror*, but I am not a child. I know there is a listening device concealed in the ceiling rose of the parlour - the fools left a tell-tale trail of plaster dust when they installed it. I could take it out. I would have to stand on a kitchen chair and stretch. I am 70 and my time in prison has left me weaker than before, so I would probably totter and break my silly neck on the parquet floor.

Serve them right.

I don't want to give them the satisfaction.

Not yet. Who knows what other eyes and ears they have hidden here? They know what I am working on. It involves power beyond their wildest dreams, yet they could never conceive of such a plan themselves.

While I still have blood in my veins and some form of a brain in my head, I must make these notes (stuck in between the pages of an old recipe book – how quaint) of what we discovered and the work to come.

If you are reading this, then I pray you are one of us. A believer.

Before those fools at Military Intelligence interrupted us, we were learning so much from my reconstruction of Crowne's experiment at Barfield. Those brave children tested and demonstrated the power of imagination to the hilt.

A power that I still contend has underrated military potential as we settle into this permafrost relationship with our former 'allies' in the East.

We could, to coin an ugly phrase, weaponise the power of reading and knowledge – if there was the will...

But we got derailed before I even got close to my aim - to connect all the streams of knowledge in the world. For there is as much power in the

135

control of knowledge as there is in the knowledge itself. Who is the gatekeeper to the library, who has the key to the safe with the confidential files, who knows where the bodies are buried? In my long and bitter experience, men, usually.

Exiled to deepest, darkest, rural Suffolk, they think that by denying me access to my precious books, my archives, I can no longer continue my research.

They could not be more wrong.

For I am planning a better way. I explained it to the girl. A new system to store every piece of information on the planet.

A system that will one day connect us all.

Who designs this system, who controls it, will shape our world for generations to come.

That is why I am determined it must be...a child.

CHAPTER 11

An Unwanted Guest

Silence hung in the fairy circle. Over the horizon, a dawn of the softest rose bloomed into life, heralded by a chorus of larks, wrens and pipits from the meadows below. Jewel couldn't be sure if she had just heard a story, or dreamed it. It had taken all night long, and Evelyn's encounter with and search for the green prince had felt so real – as if Jewel herself had been there.

She sat up and rubbed her eyes. 'And it was this same green prince who took Evie from the Unicorn?'

Thumb nodded. 'I am sure of it.'

Jewel frowned. 'But why? Had they ever met before? Did she stop trying to find him once she knew he was made of stampstone?'

'I have told you everything!' Thumb snapped. Then,

composing himself, he forced out a sharp smile. 'Why, child, you must ask the Empress herself, when you find her. Because *find the prince* and you will find Evie.'

Jewel's mind was half asleep, half in the new day. But it was stirring into frenetic life, trying to connect strands of information, join dots, trying above all to make sense of the thoughts that had torn through her mind like a ragged line of blinding electric fire when she clapped eyes on her aunt for the first ever and only time. Thoughts that had scorched her mind and soul forever.

'But she was in love with him, wasn't she?' She twisted around on her knees, imploring. 'Once she knew he was made of stampstone, maybe she was able to find him?'

'We cannot deal in maybes!' Thumb sounded furious, but Jewel detected a panic in his eyes as he searched for the right words. 'The past is the past. Right now, your aunt is in grave peril. The Librarian summoned you here. Only a Reader can save another Reader.'

'Fairies have told you what fairies know!' added a sombre Puck. 'Now gather your wits and off you go!'

'Please, not to the Ghostly Glades,' said Fizz, who had not enjoyed Thumb's story and was still cowering under his reed blanket. 'If you see a ghost, who you gonna call? Not this hamster. That's specifically why I went ex-directory.'

Thumb chuckled. 'Fear not, trembling rodent. Ghostly Glades was only where our Empress first saw the prince. It is not where stampstone is most commonly found.'

Jewel bit her lip, the true scale of the challenge facing her now becoming as clear as the white morning light bleeding through the tree tops all around. 'The Frozen Sea.'

'The Frozen Sea, we agree!' Then Puck looked embarrassed, and all the watching fairies stared hard at their clawed or cloven feet. 'Just one tiny flaw . . . we don't know how to get there any more!'

'You don't know where the Frozen Sea is?' said Jewel in exasperation. 'The edge of your world? How can that even be possible?'

Thumb sighed. 'When the Empress was compiling all the information to go on the Stampstone, she collected every map in Folio.'

'Every single map she took, every atlas, every one from every book!' added Puck miserably.

Jewel thought wistfully back to the atlas that had brought her here, wishing she had got further than the Idea Jungle, that she hadn't let the Librarian take it back . . .

'The maps were scanned and stored, so they could be continuously viewable on the stampstones, so everyone knew where they were all the time . . .'

'Apart from us,' said one of the giants miserably.

'Because you don't have stampstones?' said Jewel.

'No, because we is giants and we never has a clue where we is, do we?' She scratched her hairy chin and nudged the giant next to her hard in the ribs. 'Do we?'

Her other half snapped out of his doze, spluttering. 'What? Where is we?'

'See,' said the first giant, sagely.

'But there must be someone with a stampstone who can tell you. I mean, do you even know roughly where in Folio the Sea is, north, south . . . ?'

'Folio is a big world, my dear. It is the world of the imagination. The Frozen Sea is at the very edge of it.' He looked at his neat little feet in embarrassment. 'We just don't know which edge.'

'Are you quite sure you don't want to wear a stampstone?' said Jewel. 'It would be so helpful right now.' She got to her feet, thinking fast. At heart, she liked things to be logical. And this seemed like a puzzle with a logical solution. There was always one, if you sucked your pencil hard enough and furrowed your brow enough to give your brain space to work.

'How about the Unreads? They must still be mining the stampstone, making new ones . . .'

Thumb shook his head. 'The Stampstone is so precious and central to how Folio runs now, that access to all production processes is strictly controlled. In Evie's absence, the Bears are now in charge. And I don't think we are their favourite people at this exact moment.'

Thumb then started to further explain that once spriggans have rescued a person and brought them to an enchanted fairy circle, it isn't done to ask to go back, when there was a tremendous explosion. The air between the fairy toadstools filled with fire and light and noise, while a strange crackling echoed around the enchanted ring.

Puck leaped to his feet. 'Entry here is by my charm, which unwelcome guest makes this alarm?'

In plumes of dusty smoke and streaks of electricity, something crashed through the magic wall into the fairy ring, where it lay, twitching and sparking. The giants lumbered up, brandishing their clubs, and Jewel could see Thumb on Majesty desperately trying to rouse the spriggans from their slumber.

But she waved her hand. 'It's all right, everyone. I know who this is.'

For splayed out there in front of them all, battered, dented, and blackened, was the still just-recognisable form of the one robot Jewel had hoped she would see again.

Pandora.

Wearily, the Unread raised her head off the ground and said, 'It looks like you are trying to go on an adventure. Would you like some help with this?'

Kneeling, Jewel noticed that Pandora's copper skin was scratched by briars, and the bright light of her eyes seemed dimmer than before. But she had come to help her, as promised. Perhaps she was a friend, after all.

'How did you find me? No one is meant to know about this place.'

With great effort, Pandora leaned over and reached for Jewel's tunic collar. With her finger and thumb, she removed a small copper dot about the size of Jewel's little fingernail.

'I attached this while you were in sleeping mode,' said Pandora. 'It's a helpful tracking device, meaning your personal assistant never loses sight of you, however long the journey!'

Jewel stared at her in horror, now worried about what she had done. 'You mean you bugged me?'

'Terms and conditions apply. For full details of our privacy policy see—'

'I can't believe you actually bugged me! You're meant to be my assistant!'

There was that look, if it could be called that, on the Unread's face again. That expression which had caught her eye in the crowd by the Unicorn Monument.

'But this is why I bugged you. So I could remain your helpful personal assistant, close by at all times!'

A shadow fell across the girl and the prone robot.

'Give her to me, child. I shall dispose of this unwanted machine beyond our enchanted ring,' said one of the giants, stretching out two tree trunk sized arms.

'No, you can't!' said Jewel, standing protectively over Pandora. 'Unwanted to you maybe, but she might be our one chance. Look. Unlike you fairies, she has the one thing we need right now.' She turned to face the robot, staring at the pulsing disc in the centre of her chest. 'Pandora, can you use your stampstone to access a map, and tell us how to get to the Frozen Sea?'

'Searching for you now,' said Pandora, her eyes flickering. 'Looking for maps, and then seas . . . buffering . . .'

Then after what felt a whole further night in the fairy ring, the robotic voice at last echoed out across the silent circle. 'Location found. The Frozen Sea. Would you like to set this as a destination?'

'Yes!' everyone chorused at once.

'Setting destination . . . This journey will take approximately two and a half days of walking.'

Thumb shook his head at this. 'You must hurry. Your aunt is gravely ill. I do not know how long she has left . . . That was why she wanted to return to your world when she did.'

Jewel immediately wished Pandora hadn't told her exactly how long the journey would take. The hope that the robot's arrival had summoned within her now sharply fell, like a ship tossed upon a very unfrozen sea. Was it possible to ever know too much about things, she wondered for the first time.

The display on Pandora's stampstone flashed, the challenge written in inescapable glowing letters, somehow more compelling than if it had been engraved in rock.

TIME TO DESTINATION: 63 HOURS, APPROHIMATELY 191 MILES

'Then I guess we'll have to walk fast, won't we?' said Jewel.

* * *

The fairies gathered by the edge of their enchanted ring to wave the travellers off. Jewel now wore a special suit of fairy chainmail, like Thumb's, sewn together from what appeared to be cobwebs. It had been made by the pixies, and when they presented it to her, draped over their tiny arms, they giggled.

'Our special webmail! This will keep you safe from any blade!'

Then it was Jewel's turn to laugh. 'You are the kindest fairies I have ever met. Although I am not sure how cobwebs can protect me from a dragon.' But when she tried to pull the shirt apart, struggling with all her might, quite unable to even make a tiny tear, the pixies laughed some more. It fitted perfectly and was so light, she immediately forgot she was even wearing it.

The pixies, who admittedly had the advantage of magic, had been extremely industrious and had also made her a robe to go over the cobweb mail, sewn together from every leaf in the forest – oak, ash, beech and more. Not only was it a cloak of glorious different greens but, as they reminded her, was the best way to hide in open country.

The cloak had a deep and generous hood, deliberately made so, in which Fizz sat, fulminating with rage despite the store of acorns that one of the leprechauns had shyly slipped in there for him to feast on.

'When I find out who was responsible for booking this travel, they are going to get a very angry postcard, and when I say postcard, I actually mean a wild cat in a sack.'

Pandora stood next to Jewel, gleaming, as good as new in the morning sun. Every inch of her had been polished by the gnomes, who were very keen on housework, until they could see every hair of their very hairy faces in her burnished skin. They stood in a huddle, peering at her in wonder, until they jumped back in awe when the numbers that ran in lines all over her body began to pulse.

Puck danced forward. Hanging over his arm he had a garland of cowslips, primroses and violets, which he placed around Jewel's neck. 'Take this, our fairy necklace of wild flowers fair, for many threats and dangers, it makes you aware.'

Jewel inhaled the fresh scents and somehow felt clearer, readier for the journey ahead. Pandora scanned them and analysed the percentage of each flower in each one, and the origins of each flower and where they could be found all over the world.

'This will be terrible for my hay fever!' sneezed Fizz. 'Thanks for nothing!'

Almost unseen, a big-eared and bald house elf shyly slipped a package of dock leaves tied with a string of daisies into the pockets of Jewel's robe, rubbing his stomach with a sly smile as he did.

Finally, Thumb sailed forward from the crowd on Majesty, who dipped before the travellers. 'Thank you for undertaking this brave quest, Reader Jewel and Unread Pandora.'

'And me!' chirruped Fizz. 'Everyone always forgets the hamster. Every. Time. Would it help if I tattooed my name on your hand?'

'We wish you all luck, including you, offensive rodent. And you will need it, for your travels will be fraught with danger.'

'I know,' said Jewel. As she adjusted her fairy robe and made sure the garland sat properly around her neck, it finally dawned upon her. This was not a dream, or a movie, or a game. It was not dressing up, it was for real. Yet she could not help a small, sharp smile darting across her face as she squinted in the bright sunlight.

'But I feel less frightened than when I arrived. What you have told me makes me more determined than ever. We will find her.'

Then all the fairies and imps smothered them in

embraces and farewells, before magically vanishing behind the circle of mushrooms and toadstools, invisible to the non-fairy eye once more.

The trio were alone on the top of the meadow hill, the whole of Folio stretched out before them like a pretty patchwork quilt of springtime green and white. If Jewel squinted through one eye, it looked a bit like the Lake District viewed from the Pennines on an outward-bound hike. But then she remembered they stood on a fairy hill, her hamster could talk and was much ruder than she ever imagined, and they were relying on a robot to help them find a mysterious green prince, and the Empress of Folio.

Evelyn Hastings.

Jewel felt that flash of fire again, that connection she had felt before, deep in her heart. A connection she was growing more sure of with every second which passed.

Her face hardened. 'Pandora. Take us to the Frozen Sea.'

CHAPTER 12

The Best Route

At first the walk was easy going, following a broad path that wound itself over a series of low grassy hills like a thread, and the air was suddenly sweet with the promise of imminent summer warmth and possibility.

The ground was firm, the sky was blue and Jewel's expression blank, as it often seemed to others, but inside her feelings once more seethed like a boiling cauldron. What had she just agreed to do? Follow a robot to the edge of this land, to a frozen sea, where she would almost certainly face a terrifying dragon and his stampstone rider. All for an aunt she'd never even met.

'I'm not even related to her,' said Jewel, and suddenly stopped in the middle of the track so abruptly that Fizz flew out of her hood and on to the ground. Up ahead,

Pandora automatically stopped at the unexpected noise, turning around.

'Well that was fun,' said Fizz, painfully. 'Can we do that again, please, and by again I mean, are you trying to actually kill me?'

Jewel crouched down and tenderly picked him up, stroking the shivering, dust-covered creature.

'I have never wanted to kill anyone or anything less in my life. That's why I want to know, is this worth it? We could both get killed.'

'She's your aunt, isn't she? Hamsters have a lot of aunts. We would have stuck together, but . . .' He gave a sad shrug. There were some things that even Fizz couldn't joke about.

'Adopted aunt. And I'm not a hamster.'

'Patricia's sister, though. You love Patricia, don't you?'

Jewel nodded, biting her lip. She did, very much. Patricia had cared for her, taught her, read to her, hours and hours after school, at weekends . . . A cold thought flickered at the back of her mind, an unwelcome blast of daylight. *It was Patricia's fault she was so different.*

That was why she knew more words than other children her age, why she could work out Latin numerals, why she knew there were eight species of bear. Patricia, and her

150

home teaching! Well, she hadn't asked to be different. Being different had made her life a misery.

She stared at her lengthening shadow in the bright white dust.

Who did she truly owe something to?

Who was worth facing a dragon for?

Another shadow joined hers. 'Hi! Is there a problem? Would you like to make an authorised waypoint or terminate the journey here?'

Jewel stood up slowly and looked once more into the electric-blue eyes of the copper robot.

'Do you know who you are, Pandora?'

'I am Pandora, your personal Unread assistant, number LH1951.'

Jewel shook her head. 'That's not what I meant. I know *what* you are. But who are you, really? Why are you helping us, for example? Who do you owe something to?'

The robot's face stayed flat. 'I do not understand the question. I am your assigned personal assistant. I am here to help!'

Jewel stayed silent, looking at Pandora. But her gaze was focused on the distant mountains ahead, where billowing white clouds were pierced by sharp snow-capped peaks. They looked cold, severe and unwelcoming. Beyond them surely lay the icy sea they were headed for.

She knew she could just turn around now. Find a book somewhere, any book, go home . . .

This was Folio's problem. Not hers. Evie was Patricia's sister – why didn't *she* come here and rescue her? If it mattered that much, the Librarian looked powerful enough to find a way.

Yet she couldn't turn back.

Every cell in her body seemed united in a conspiracy against her. *Walk on*, they seemed to urge. *Keep going. Find the sea. Save her.*

'Helping is OK,' whispered Fizz in her ear, as if he could read her mind too. 'Helping is good.'

'I know!' said Jewel. 'I just wish I knew why.'

Except deep down, she knew exactly why. She just wasn't ready to admit it yet.

As if in response, there was a sudden flapping noise behind them, and she whipped around. But there was nothing to see, only the blue sky behind them, the fairy hill fading into the distance. Perhaps it was just her fairy robe, caught by the breeze.

So they walked on.

As they strode, Pandora provided a running commentary. 'That is a blackberry bush. Here are fifteen great things to do with blackberries that doctors don't even know about . . . Walking fast? Is it time you got your blood pressure checked? . . . Are you on a quest? Heroes who took this path also went on these quests. Why not check them out? There is one with a voyage, one with a horse, and one with a prince too!'

Fairy fields and brooks soon gave way to an overgrown track. Pandora walked ahead with purpose, never wavering a second, slicing through the undergrowth with mechanical efficiency. She didn't need to stop to rest, or to eat, or to drink, and sometimes needed to be reminded that the others did.

'Pandora!' said Jewel, flushed with exhaustion and slumping on to a lichen-flecked boulder. 'Wait! I can't go as fast as you.'

The robot jerked to a halt and turned around. 'Remember, when hiking in open country, always take regular rest breaks, stay out of the sun, and make sure you drink enough water!'

'Yes, thanks Mum,' said Jewel, carefully unwrapping the dock leaf parcel the house elf had slipped in her robe pocket.

'I am not your mother.'

'You do a good impression.' Inside the neat little parcel

were some honey cakes smelling faintly of saffron. Jewel took a bite and offered some to Fizz as well.

'A mother is a woman in relation to her children.'

'Does it need to be a woman?' said Fizz between mouthfuls. 'My mother was a hamster.'

'Yes, thank you both, I know what a mother is! Who my mother is! What she is!' said Jewel.

You don't know who your birth mother is, or your father, though, do you? said the voice in her head, but she once more ignored it, wrapped up the remaining cakes, and tightened her robe.

A shadow fell over them.

Her fairy flower garland of violets began to glow and vibrated lightly against her chest. She glanced up to see an imperial oculis, one of the Stampstone's eyes, hovering directly above. It had been harder to see in the dark before, and now in daylight, Jewel could see the roving eye in all its dark, sinister splendour.

The black skin had the stretched, gelatinous appearance of an eyeball that was all iris and no white. It floated lower and lower towards them.

'Pandora! Watch out!'

They fled down the path towards a ragged copse of trees. This did not stop the oculis floating ominously over the treetops. As ever, Pandora did not seem disturbed by anything, even this glistening black orb that now poked through the leaves above their heads.

'It is recording our position,' Pandora noted. 'The Vice Regent will now be aware of our location.'

'So shouldn't we hide?' Jewel said, her eyes not leaving the orb.

'We cannot hide from the Stampstone.'

The eye hummed loudly and Jewel braced herself, fearing the worst, but then with a queasy roll, the floating spy spun around and moved on in search of new subjects.

'It won't be long before it returns,' said Jewel. 'And perhaps, next time, with some less friendly robots. Pandora, you need to find us a quicker route, as fast as you can.'

Pandora started searching for the best route again, and they walked on further among the trees that were growing darker as the day lengthened. But not so dark that Jewel couldn't see the path forking in two ahead, and two wooden signs on a pole pointing in either direction.

'Uh oh,' said Fizz.

'Pandora,' called Jewel. 'We've found a signpost.'

Pandora came striding through the bracken towards them. 'Toy Town,' she read from the first sign, and then from the other one, 'Monster Marsh.'

'Well, that settles it,' said Fizz, rubbing his paws together. 'Off to Toy Town we go. Sounds like my kind of town. They might even have a car small enough for me to drive.'

Jewel waved him quiet. 'So Toy Town,' she said to Pandora, 'is where all—'

'The fictional toys in stories live, correct. Why not call in on the Velveteen Rabbit for tea? Or watch a show at Pinocchio's Puppet Theatre?'

'I get it. And . . . Monster Marsh . . . ?'

'. . . is where all fictional monsters live. Never approach during the hours of darkness, please only visit with an approved guide and take suitable protective measures at all times. Not suitable for children.'

'That was a close shave,' said Jewel. 'How far is it to Toy Town?

'About two hours at the current pace . . . the stampstone is suggesting a better and faster route through Monster Marsh.'

Fizz shook his head in disbelief. A silence settled in the copse, like falling rain. 'That's a pretty funny joke, for a robot. And by funny, I mean look at my face.' He stared stonily at the Unread, who stared equally stonily back.

'It was not a humorous remark,' said Pandora. 'Our best

route is through Monster Marsh, one hundred per cent.'

'Pandora,' said Jewel. 'Nobody ever, in the history of map reading, said the best route must be through somewhere called Monster Marsh. Especially when it's getting dark!'

Pandora blinked. 'Recalculating . . . The stampstone still suggests we take the path to Monster Marsh.'

'I don't believe this,' said Fizz. 'Look at that path there! Right in front of us! With a sign! It goes to Toy Town! Action Men and Barbies! Which I like to chew in equal measure, by the way! Why are you making us go somewhere that actually has monster in the title?'

'The Stampstone knows everything,' said Pandora. 'It would not give incorrect information.'

'Maybe she's right, Fizz,' said Jewel. 'What do we know? Maybe Monster Marsh isn't as bad as it sounds?'

'It could literally not sound any worse!'

Jewel frowned. Every instinct in her body agreed with Fizz. She had a vision of Toy Town in her head already – the brightly coloured houses, white fences and friendly characters waving from their pretty gardens. It would be like walking into a Noddy cartoon or a Rupert Bear annual. And Monster Marsh . . . well, that just made her shiver.

The hamster flopped back into her hood with a sigh of

exasperation as Jewel and Pandora set off down the steep path, grabbing on to the slender young trees for support as they stumbled between them. Before too long, they emerged on to a large plain of marshland that stretched out to where the land met the late afternoon sky in clumps of spiky reeds.

To Jewel's immense relief, it appeared to be entirely deserted. There was no eye in the sky, either.

'No monsters so far!' she said with a forced smile.

'I'm staying in your hood, and by hood, I mean reinforced panic room,' said Fizz, burrowing down into its folds as deep as he could.

They walked on in silence, save for the splashing of their feet in the boggy ground, and Jewel's odd muted cry when she stumbled and slipped, fumbling for a grassy tussock to stop her falling face down in the mud. Wiping her hands on her robe, she noticed that the fairy garland of violets was beginning to very faintly pulse with dim light. Was there danger up ahead?

'Wait! I'm getting a bad feeling about this.'

Pandora stopped. She was some distance ahead and there was a spray of mud on both her copper legs, as if she had been lightly dipped in the ground, but she showed no other signs of exertion or stress.

'Be sure to wear waterproof clothing when walking in marshland.'

Jewel shook her head. When she had arrived in Folio, the Unreads and the stampstones had dazzled her with their science-fiction brilliance. It had felt too good to be true. Now she was beginning to suspect it was.

They continued their up and down progress across the marsh, Jewel taking sharper breaths as the ground got less and less solid. Dark clouds clustered over the sky like flies, until every ray of sun was blocked from view, the reeds and grass turning slate grey in the dull light.

Jewel shivered and the garland glowed again. This time, the light was brighter and the flowers pulsed harder against her chest.

She looked around. Fairytale Valley lay far behind them now and they were quite alone, apart from the odd dragonfly darting in and out of the tall reeds.

And yet . . . something was making the hairs on the back of her neck prick up.

Something, somewhere, stirred beneath Jewel's feet.

The muddy dip they stood in began to bubble, air popping up here and there with gentle plops.

Jewel looked down. The garland was going into overdrive.

'Pandora. When you said this was where fictional monsters live, where exactly did you mean?'

'Exact location unknown.'

Jewel looked around them, at the marsh which lay as if flattened by a fist, the life crushed out of it. Far off in the reeds, a crow cawed and there was a sharp crack of wings as it soared off towards the brooding clouds. She looked behind her, either side, and up in the sky. This marshland was mysterious, but there was one thing she could say.

'It's empty, Pandora. I can see as far as the horizon in nearly every direction, and there's no one here! There is nothing to see, just a single bird, and now that's flown off into the sky too. Where are they all?'

Across the marsh there was the sound of mud splitting and popping in the early evening air.

'I do not understand the question.'

'The monsters from every story ever told. They have to live in this marsh, you said. But I can't see any. So. Where. Did. They. Go?'

'Searching . . . No further information available.'

Then Pandora suddenly listed to the side as one of her copper legs was pulled beneath the mud.

'You know you said you looked everywhere?' said

Fizz. 'Did you include *underneath* us?'

Something grabbed at Jewel's ankles, twisted and caked in soil.

And she started to run.

CHAPTER 13

Monster Marsh

All around them, the marsh erupted. Mud exploded into the air, as if from a geyser, showering the travellers as they stumbled from ditch to ditch, lunging for reed clumps to steady them as they ran. Quite without warning, bomb-like craters gave way under their feet. Pandora strode purposefully, Jewel following in a breathless scramble, then the ground disappeared, and she fell, grasping at stalks. Blistered hands and claws were pulling at her feet, her cloak dragging her down . . .

She was almost too scared to turn around and see what they were, but glancing behind, there was just a glimpse of bone and nail, scratching at her legs.

'I thought monsters were made up,' gasped Fizz.

'They feel pretty real to me,' muttered Jewel, hauling

herself free of yet another decaying hand.

The hands became arms which wriggled upwards out of the ground, dragging shoulders and then the tops of heads behind them. As light faded to night, the monsters of Monster Marsh arose, casting grotesque shadows over the land.

A vampire, with cape and talon-fingered arms flung wide. A fur covered wolfwoman that stalked on her hind legs, claws emerging from her fingertips as she ran. A moaning mummy trailing bandages, a swamp creature . . . The most famous monsters of legend were all here.

'Recalculating route,' called back Pandora as she ran, her stampstone flashing. 'Please select option. Walking or public transport?'

'Is running an option?' said Jewel, kicking off another decaying zombie hand that disintegrated as her foot made contact.

'No other route available,' said Pandora, now reversing, cornered by a freakishly large ape beating his chest.

'That would appear so,' said Jewel, being driven slowly towards her by a group of pale children with outstretched arms and hollow eyes. Their heads lolled listlessly to the side, as if their necks had been snapped clean in half.

'Is it safe to come out yet, and by safe, I mean are we back at home under the duvet with a Curly Wurly and reading *The Beano* by torchlight?' whimpered a voice from her hood.

'Not exactly,' said Jewel. And she was right. From every side, the grisly underground residents of Monster Marsh lurched towards them, groaning softly like wind in the trees. They moved in unsteady unison, on scaled feet and legs still wrapped with chains. The encircling crowd ran six layers deep.

They were anything but safe.

They were surrounded.

Jewel jumped as one of the monsters read his stampstone screen and suddenly lurched forward. The creature was a swollen, disfigured mess of skin and stiches. Dressed in rags, his eyes were at different heights, his mouth crooked, his nose not much more than a hole in his face. His arms were entirely different colours and lengths, raised out in front of him as if they were held there by wires, and with one hand missing a thumb. As his legs were also different lengths, he walked at an angle.

He appeared to be completely sewn together. Swinging the glare of his stampstone across them like a lantern, he growled. 'Who?'

Jewel blanched. 'My name is Reader Jewel Hastings, and this my tireless assistant Pandora, and this my fearless companion Fizz.' The monster gave a grunt of disinterest. 'And you must be—'

'Frankenstein!'

Fizz spoke from behind her ear. 'I don't mean to be rude, big guy, but I always thought that was the name of the scientist, not the monster?'

'Silence!' roared the creature. A heavy hand shot out, grabbed Jewel by the neck, and lifted her clean off the ground with Fizz clinging on to her hair by a single paw. 'Or I break.'

'Please,' gasped Jewel, her hands around his thick fingers, trying to prise them apart. 'We don't mean any harm. We only seek to find—'

'The Frozen Sea?' said Frankenstein, letting them fall, sprawling, into the mud.

'It is curious,' said Jewel, as calmly as she could, rubbing her neck, 'how everyone here seems to know my business almost before I do.'

'Yeah, why not pick on someone your own size, greenie,' snarled Fizz.

By way of answer, Frankenstein crouched down. Even at half height, he towered over her. He showed her his stampstone with a grunt.

A wave of images and text scrolled past, a jumble of

headlines, reports and photos from something called The Library Noticeboard, which Jewel assumed was the Folio news service. But there were also videos with captions and comments attached. Whatever the form, the content was the same, repeated in different ways, over and over again.

READER WANTED IN CONNECTION WITH EMPRESS DISAPPEARANCE

FUGITIVE JEWEL SPOTTED HEADING FOR FROZEN SEA: REWARD OFFERED

KNIGHT ON DRAGON IS MADE-UP NEWS, SAYS TALKING BEAR

Jewel's eyes glowed with the reflection of a thousand scrolling words and pictures. Glowed, and then glazed over, as she could not begin to comprehend what she was seeing. Thumb had explained how the Vice Regent wanted her as an easy scapegoat and that an oculis had spotted them . . . but 'made-up' news?

'That's impossible. Every citizen of Folio was there! We all saw it. There was a dragon . . . a knight made of stampstone . . . they took the Empress!'

The watching monsters gave a low gurgle of amusement.

'I am the Mummy!' cried out the Mummy, thrusting her bandaged wrists towards the intruders.

'Why we believe you, leetle girl?' sneered the vampire, showing his stampstone. A video began to play, but as soon as Jewel saw what it was, she turned away.

She could avoid the picture but she could not avoid the sound. The roar of the dragon, the screams of agony from his burning victims, the cry of anguish from Evie as she was swept off into the night. It was like her aunt was being kidnapped all over again as the video filmed by those in the audience at the Unicorn spooled on and on.

When it had at last finished, a horrified silence fell over the marsh. Deep inside her, Jewel felt a line had been crossed. Abducting someone and killing people in front of a crowd was bad enough, but to watch it on a screen, like a movie or a TV ad, made her feel even more powerless and guilty.

At least it was proof, surely – incontrovertible proof that she had nothing to do with Evie's abduction. She was trying to save her! She would never harm—

But the vampire was grinning, showing his dripping canines.

'There is not so much to do down below the ground during the day. We have watched this video thousands of times!'

'So you must have seen that I wasn't involved in any way! You can see . . . there was a dragon! A knight! How could I even begin to make those things appear?'

'Don't ask Count Dracula, leetle girl!' said the vampire. 'Ask the rest of ze audience who vere vatching.'

On his stampstone, he showed her the comments left under the video. Jewel didn't recognise all the names, and some of them were little more than numbers or codes, but the meaning of their words was all too clear.

Unread 6317 2 days ago
Dragon definitely a hologram. Vice Regent confirmed it and a bear would never lie!!!

BoyWhoCryWolf85 1 day ago
I saw a Reader on the night, screaming and shouting. Suspicious much?

Unreads4ever 1 day ago
Typical Reader. Nothing but trouble. Good riddance!

Emperors_New_Clothes 2 weeks ago

Hey guys why not check out my latest outfit?
New vids up now!

PinocchioRulesOK 1 day ago

You can't believe anything these days IMO

Now Jewel was not just disbelieving, but bewildered. None of this made sense.

'This is insane,' she said. 'How can people just make something up, a completely different version of what actually happened in front of my own eyes, with no evidence, and everyone believes it?'

'Everybody same everywhere,' slurred Frankenstein. 'People always prefer good story to truth! And I should know!' He staggered towards her. 'So now we hand you to Bear for reward. You make Empress disappear.'

Jewel took a slippery step back.

'Even if I could, which is impossible, why would I kidnap my own . . . aunt? And where is she? In my pocket?'

Dracula hissed in her ear. 'We don't need reasons, leetle girl.' He tapped his stampstone. 'This tells us all we need to know.'

'And if it told you to jump off a cliff, would you?'

169

A silence fell across the marsh. The thick grey clouds parted and Jewel got a better glimpse of her captors. For some reason she suddenly felt a pang of sympathy. They didn't look so scary after all. Frankenstein, sewn together from different bits, his sackcloth trousers several inches too short, flapping in the breeze. Dracula's cape had moth holes and was trailing in the bog. The Werewoman had bald patches, and the Mummy was more mud than bandages.

Werewoman howled at her in rage, baring her fangs.

The Mummy said once more, with emphasis, 'I am the Mummy!'

Frankenstein jabbed Jewel in the chest. 'Why you think we here?'

'Do you believe any of us vant to leeve in zis godforsaken swamp?' said Dracula.

Behind him, the creature from the Black Lagoon gave a fishy shrug with his fins. 'I do!'

'Apart from you!' snapped the vampire.

But the swamp creature had put a thought into Jewel's head. 'Pandora! Look up Monster Marsh for me.'

Lights pulsed over her assistant's body for a moment, and then, 'Searching for Monster Marsh,' said Pandora. 'I have found over ten thousand mentions on the Stampstone.

There are many complaints about monster behaviour. There is another item about a rigorous health and safety risk assessment, and finally an official recommendation that all monsters be restricted to the Marsh.'

'Why?'

Pandora recited the list. '"Monster behaviour includes, but is not limited to, feeding on the blood of the innocent, luring travellers to their doom, terrifying the unwary. In a survey conducted by the Folio Federation via the Stampstone, these behaviours received a two-star or less rating from other citizens."'

'So they have to live in this wasteland because everyone's scared of them? I can see why! Sneaking up on us like that. Who do you think you are?'

'I am the Mummy!' said the Mummy despondently, looking at the ground.

'Just because I made from other people's bodies. You think you more clever,' said Frankenstein. 'And you think you better too,' he added. He didn't sound gruff or scary. He sounded hurt.

That caught Jewel. She knew what it was like when people made you feel inferior to them, for any reason. And, looking at them – these monsters, twitching over their glowing stampstones in the pale moonlight – she felt a wave of shame wash through her.

They were only monsters, after all. She hardly knew anything about them either, it was true.

'You're right,' she replied, feeling very abashed. 'I'm sorry.'

The monsters shook their heads doubtfully. 'Your aunt vas deefferent,' said Dracula. 'She fought for monster equality. She understood us, leetle girl.'

Jewel looked at the line of monsters, and now saw only one thing in their green-tinged eyes as they shakily drew closer, hands outstretched . . .

Hunger. They were starving.

Here they all were, quite alone in this desolate marsh, miles from anywhere. What did they live on? In the absence of any other food source, it looked like she and Fizz were the only items on the menu.

She glanced up at the brooding sky, hoping she might glimpse the Librarian, but saw only clouds flitting across a pitiless moon. For a moment, she thought she heard again the flapping noise that she had heard on the track from Puck's Hill, but then it was gone . . . and next, by some miracle, she had an idea.

Jewel delved deep into her robe pockets and brought out the last of the honey cakes that the house elf had given her, proffering them on her open palm to the monsters.

Fizz spoke out of the side of his mouth. 'Are you sure you want to do that?' he said. 'They're our last ones.'

'Quite sure,' said Jewel. Then, to the monsters, 'Go on! Don't be shy. They taste much better than me, I promise. You look like you could do with them.'

With a lurch forward, Frankenstein stretched out his hand. 'For me?' he slurred.

'For you. For you all.'

His eyes melted. 'No one ever give anything nice to monsters before.'

Then he took a large, crumbling bite, and a warm smile of satisfaction spread over his face. Carefully, he halved one of the cakes, and offered a piece to Dracula. The vampire took a suspicious nibble, but then he too gave a broad smile, something Jewel had not yet seen him do. Then the Werewoman was gobbling chunks of cake down greedily. The Swamp Monster was trying to eat his slice with webbed fingers and not drop too many crumbs. The Mummy bolted hers. 'I am the Mummy!' she said with a sigh of contentment.

When the last of the cakes had been shared and devoured by their monster captors, they all turned to their prisoner.

'Thank you!' slurred Frankenstein.

'Not so frightening after all,' said Jewel. 'Just hungry. Do you trust me more now?'

'We do, brave leetle girl, we do,' said Dracula, and he sounded almost wistful, as if he wanted to say more.

Then all their eyes flashed green, as if on a signal, and the ground beneath their feet began to roar and tremble, the topsoil vibrating like the skin of a drum. Muddy furrows under the monsters cracked apart, slowly but irrevocably widening into chasms, into which they sunk, moaning all the while as their underground lair reclaimed them.

'Wait!' cried Jewel. 'Won't you help us?'

Frankenstein looked at Dracula, who shook his head.

'Please!' said Jewel. 'Help us defeat the green prince. He has taken the Empress who listened to you . . .'

The monsters were disappearing beneath the earth, the ground closing over them, then the night filled with a shuddering roar!

'Wait!'

Frankenstein jammed the walls of mud open for a moment with his huge green fists.

'You never defeat green prince. Impossible. He control everything.'

A shock ran through him, making him spasm with pain,

and he cried out in agony.

Jewel crouched over the edge. 'What do you mean? What just happened?'

'He send pain through stone . . .' gasped the monster through gritted teeth. 'He see everything. Know everything. Only one thing defeat him!'

'Tell me!'

'Remember . . . what you are.'

Then with a scream that seemed hollowed out from the dark cavern below, he let the marsh close back over him. Jewel watched in fascinated horror, and the last thing she saw was Frankenstein's disfigured hand, reaching one last time for the sky, the stampstone sewn into his wrist still bright with a blurred electronic green as it sank beneath the earth.

The Magician Project – Extract 45
(KV 4/1999-14)
Magazine Article, Barfield House Sale,
1961

COUNTRY LIFE, WEDNESDAY 19th JULY 1961

Upon instructions from HM Government, Wadley
and Wools will Sell by Auction the residual
contents of Barfield Hall, Barfield, nr
Salisbury, Wiltshire on the premises.

The contents have been temporarily removed to
The Wadley and Wools Auction Rooms in
Salisbury for cataloguing and security.

Furnishings include Art Deco Marcel Charreau
sofa and chairs (1928), artworks include
Victor Lakovsky 'Meditations On' series (1-
V111, oils), 'Still Life of Hounds with Game'
(J. Masterson, 1797) and a 16th century
portrait in oils of Sir Nicholas Crowne, the
early modern magus, artist unknown.

Other notable entries in this sale include a 1945 Armstrong Siddeley Lancaster, pre-select gearbox, in excellent order throughout, one previous careful owner.

But perhaps the most extraordinary lot in this auction is an unrivalled collection of over 90,000 books, manuscripts and ephemera, making up Nicholas Crowne's renowned collection, once reputed to be the most extensive private library in Europe, dating back to the sixteenth century. Regrettably, owing to the size of the collection, and following strict instructions from HM Government that it be broken up, this is only available for purchase in separate lots. Any items not sold will be disposed of for security reasons.

END SECURITY FILE

CHAPTER 14

The Mountain of Strange Thoughts

The travellers slept where they fell, huddled together on the grey marsh, Pandora warming them as best she could – which wasn't very well.

'It looks like your body temperature is falling to a critical level,' she said cheerily. 'Would you like emergency lifesaving medical assistance? I regret I am unable to offer this feature at the current time.'

The cold leached through the ground into Jewel's bones, and she tossed and turned, caught between the bumpy marsh and the unforgiving metal of the robot, all the while trying not to smother the soft hamster snoring in her hood.

When sleep came upon her, in fitful waves, it was accompanied by equally unsettling dreams. She was lost

in a labyrinth, or wandering an empty mansion, or trying to navigate the playing squares of an oversized board game. In every scenario, she encountered robots, or fairies, or monsters. They either helped or hindered her, and their choices were anything but predictable.

Yet however she interacted with them, whichever choices she made, the ending of the game was always the same.

A path, or tunnel, or steps, leading to a cave of deepest dark.

Then, a winding neck snaking out, reptilian eyes blinking . . .

The pink gums exposed, dripping jaws stretched wide . . .

And everything disappeared in blinding emerald fire . . .

She sat up, her heart racing.

Blinking in the early white dawn, she saw that Pandora was no longer lying with them, but standing apart, a silhouette gazing into the rising sun. She had her hands on her hips and, for a robot personal assistant, seemed verging on thoughtful.

'Pandora?' called Jewel hesitantly, unsure whether to interrupt her.

The robot whirled around, her pale blue eyes full of

fury, which evaporated into blank nothing as soon as she registered Jewel.

'It looks like you are waking up. Would you like some breakfast?'

'Yes, very much, but we don't have any food.'

'Would it help if I described some delicious breakfast items instead?'

'Not really, but thanks.'

Jewel flopped back on to the mud, Fizz groggily crawling out in the nick of time to avoid being squashed by her. She was troubled, and not only by the frightening dreams. The monsters had wanted to eat them, and then just like that, they had descended back to their subterranean lair. Frankenstein had tried to help her, but it was as if the Stampstone itself was stopping him. What on earth did he mean, 'Remember what you are?' And how did he know?

Only one thing was for sure.

The nearer they got to the Frozen Sea, the less and less sense things made.

Pandora's stampstone was pulsing. 'Recommence route?' she said. 'Time to destination, approximately thirty-six hours.'

There was no going back. For Jewel knew, in her heart, that to settle the thoughts which disturbed her both at home and in this strange land, to answer the questions which crowded her mind, both awake and asleep, questions which had only sharpened their intensity since that night at the Unicorn, when she thought she saw . . . There was only one way forward, to the only place she would find the answers she so urgently sought.

The Frozen Sea, and whatever terrors awaited there.

From the watery marsh they tracked a little river, which rose steeply into the hills towards its mountain source. There was no convenient path alongside, but a demanding bank of rough rocks and boulders. The two girls had to stoop and clamber, rather than walk, and the higher they climbed, the tougher it became. Pandora never slowed down, or even needed to rest. Jewel discovered she quite liked having a companion who never complained and who could answer any question in the world. Even if she was only a robot.

'And to think we could have been having Carrot Daiquiris with Noddy and Rupert Bear by their swimming pool in Toy Town,' said Fizz wistfully, as he was jolted in the fairy hood with Jewel's every step on the rough stones.

Pandora tapped her stampstone. 'Noddy lives with Big Ears and currently has no access to a swimming pool.

181

Rupert Bear lives with his parents in Nutwood, a suburb of Toy Town, and currently has no access to a swimming pool. The sale of cocktails is prohibited in Toy Town.'

'You know what I like most about robots?' said Fizz. 'Their sense of humour.'

'Would you like to hear a joke?' said Pandora.

'That depends,' said Fizz.

'What's brown and sticky?'

'I don't know,' said Fizz reluctantly. 'Please tell me, Pandora, what's brown and sticky?'

'A stick!'

'Like I said . . .' sighed Fizz.

The river they were following now narrowed into a sluggish stream of sorts, sullenly snaking its way ahead through the boulders. A commotion from around the next corner put Jewel on guard, but her garland remained dull and still. Even so, she braced herself as a rowing boat splashed into view, only relaxing when she saw the passengers.

There was a besuited mole reclining in the back, his head bent over his glowing stampstone, while a water vole in a natty waistcoat pulled hard at the oars. Occasionally the mole's free paw would absent-mindedly slide out, and help itself to a sandwich or slice of cold ham from the laden wicker picnic hamper that lay open between them.

'Oh really,' said the water vole. 'Must you!'

'What?' said the mole in a distracted faraway voice.

'Must you spend the whole picnic gazing at that wretched thing?'

'Umm,' said the mole, tapping his stampstone once or twice.

'Are you even listening to me, my dear fellow?'

'Oh yes,' said the mole, never lifting his eyes from the glowing screen. 'Every word.'

'Then where are we going?'

'Not sure,' muttered the mole, and as he said this – his companion now as distracted as he – the boat careered into a bank with a shudder. The oars shot out of their rowlocks and the water vole flew forward into the hamper, re-emerging with the remains of a cream sponge on his snout. He scowled at the mole.

'I'll tell you where we're going. Home! Right now!'

'Oh! But our adventure was only just beginning . . .'

The water vole ground his teeth and shook his whiskers free of cream, before restoring the oars to their rightful home. Then the boat staggered erratically on, its occupants seemingly oblivious to the party watching them from the bank.

'Do you think they're meant to be up here?' said Jewel. 'Rowing a boat down a mountain stream?'

Pandora strode on, never wanting to pause. 'Negative.' Her stampstone pulsed. 'Citizens identified as Mole and Ratty, inhabitants of Talking Animal Towers.'

'Animals that talk! Like me!' said Fizz. 'Outrageous! An infringement of copyright. I shall ask my lawyer to send them a strongly worded letter, and when I say letter, I mean a warrant for their execution!'

'Are the Talking Towers nearby?'

'Searching. Talking Animal Towers is 200 miles from here. Would you like to—'

'No,' said Jewel, frowning. 'I'm just puzzled as to why they were looking for a picnic spot amongst all these rocks. They weren't just lost . . . they didn't even seem to notice how lost they were. Where are we anyway?'

'We are in the Mountains of Mythia, home to gods, mythical beings and legends.'

'That sounds relaxing,' said Fizz. 'Any chance we could ever go anywhere not full of terrifying and powerful creatures?'

'This remains the best available route at this time,' said Pandora, stubbornly.

Jewel crouched and scooped some brackish water up

from the stream to wash her face, and froze. There was that flapping noise again. She had heard it on the way from Puck's Hill to Monster Marsh, and just before she gave the monsters the cake, and now here it was again.

Jewel turned around. Was that a flash of scarlet? Perhaps some exotic bird? She scanned the sky and saw an oculis far above them, rotating darkly. It was only a matter of time before the Vice Regent caught up with them. But surely his floating camera wasn't making the noise?

The mountains fell silent again, the only other sound coming from her empty and roaring stomach. If they didn't get something to eat soon, the chances of her and Fizz making it as far as the Frozen Sea were very remote. The oculis could watch all it wanted. They were going to fail all by themselves, without any help from their pursuers.

'Pandora, do you think these gods might have any food?'

'Our route takes us directly past their residence. One moment, please, searching for food options at The Gathering of the Gods . . . It has a one-star rating. Here is a typical review: "This may be the legendary residence of celestial deities, omnipotent, omniscient and worshipped since the dawn of time, but the indifferent food and, frankly, casual service left my wife and I wondering why we bothered."'

Poking out of the hood, Fizz shrugged. 'I'm a hamster. I'm not so bothered about the service. Let's go, my metal friend.'

Without another word, Pandora scrambled to the top of a last cluster of huge boulders and beckoned them to follow.

As the landscape beyond came into view, it was as if a page had been ripped from a book. The soft dales, meadows and woodland-lined valleys of the journey behind them were no more, and instead, they faced an ashen plateau, bordered by rocky slopes that rose up on either side into sharp peaks, with a bitter wind sweeping in between.

They were approaching the mountains she had seen from the friendly shires of Fairytale Valley. The Frozen Sea and whatever the green prince had in store for them lay beyond. Folio may have been a world of the imagination, but this felt all too real.

For a moment she closed her eyes and imagined curling up with Patricia on the sofa at home, sharing a book together, to try and steady her nerves. But as she did, Patricia's image in her mind started to become fainter, as if she was being pulled away from her.

Jewel opened her eyes and blinked. She had to focus.

A wave of heat waffled up from the barren plain ahead.

Perhaps it was the exhaustion, perhaps it was the hunger . . .

'Are you OK, kid?' whispered Fizz.

She nodded, biting her lip, but it was no good, the tears were already slipping hot and fast down her cheeks, her shoulders shuddering.

'I'm sorry,' she said, 'I keep trying to be brave, but it's just so hard . . . I feel so alone.'

'You're not alone.' His brown brow furrowed. 'Listen, I'm not a soppy kind of hamster. If you ever find me even being close to mushy, you leave me in the nearest shoebox on the side of the road, understand?'

Jewel nodded.

'And I'm not grateful for you saving me from those jerks at school. I had the situation totally under control till you barged in. All the same . . . what I'm trying to say is, you're not alone, and never will be while I'm around, OK?'

A half smile crept up one side of her weepy face.

'But I don't think that's the real reason you're crying, is it?' said Fizz.

She shook her head, unable to speak.

'You saw something that night at the Unicorn, didn't you?' He paused. Jewel did not meet his gaze. 'You don't think she's your aunt at all, do you?'

Jewel wiped her eyes on her tunic sleeve, and gently but firmly placed Fizz back in her hood.

'Come on,' she said. 'Enough of that. Let's keep up with Pandora, or we'll starve to death.'

CHAPTER 15

Gathering of the Gods

The two girls, one human, one robot, were two tiny figures crossing the plain, black strokes of ink against a vast desert plateau, dwarfed by the shadowy slopes of the mountains, swooping up in crescents of cool grey to the snowline.

The desert was dotted with vast ruins, foreshortened stumps of mighty stone pillars, toppled and crumbling. Golden towers, emblazoned with ornate carvings of animals and faces, glistered dimly in the sun, through the spots of black tarnish that crept over them like mould. Once mighty totem poles leaned to one side, their shaky foundations in the loose, dry earth slipping away. A huge wooden vaulted hall had a hole in the rafters, ravens flocking around the edge with harsh caws.

As she trekked past them, her head craned in wonder,

Jewel began to recognise these decaying structures from some of the favourite books Patricia had given her: hardback histories of different civilisations, packed with intricately detailed illustrations.

Jewel liked to stare at these pictures for hours, lying on her front in her bedroom, head in her hands, feet waving in the air. She would stare at them till the light changed from day to dark, putting her fingers in her ears, ignoring shouts from Patricia to come down for tea. The Vikings, Egyptians, the Romans – Jewel had studied them all.

She knew these were structures from different cultures – from ancient Greece to native America. They were much bigger than she ever imagined. But why were they all so empty and neglected?

However, these ruins were as nothing to what she saw next. A colossal pair of gates jutting out from the middle of the mighty plain. Two huge horns curved out of the ground to form these gates, springing as smoothly as from a bull's head. They arced right up to the sky, tips glinting.

One horn was golden and the other was white as ivory, quite smooth, like a bar of soap. And in their curves sat two heavy doors of bronze, divided into carved panels. From either side of the horns, a tall stockade of sharpened logs ran right round, enclosing whatever lay behind. Gentle curls of smoke rose from beyond the stockade.

Pandora, always far ahead, calmly came to a halt in front of the gates.

'You don't sweat, you're not out of breath,' panted Jewel, finally reaching her. 'Why are you so perfect?'

'Perfection is very much in the eye of the beholder,' said Pandora. 'I have my faults.'

'Such as?'

The robot went silent, her number lights shimmering quietly. 'I cannot feel things the way you do,' she said. 'I do not see or experience the world in the same way as you describe. I see only facts. Only data has meaning for me. I learn from experience but it does not change me. At least . . .'

Jewel stared hard at her. 'Go on,' she said, and for some reason, she felt her heart pounding.

Before Pandora could reply, the horn and ivory gates swung open with a long, drawn out groan. Jewel put her hand to her mouth in astonishment, gazing up at a towering world of giant creatures. Inhabitants, buildings, objects, all much bigger than in her own world.

Jewel checked her garland, but the flowers, while alert,

were not pulsing like they had been in Monster Marsh. She dared to relax for a moment, and breathed in the air of the gods' lair. She inhaled the hot sweet smell of candied fruit sizzling in cauldrons, and fragrant spices slathered over vegetables roasting in the sun.

There was food here, all right. But how could they get to it?

A giant centaur clopped down the cobbled street in front of them, making the ground shake under the travellers' feet. This bare-chested bearded man grew out of a horse's body as smoothly as Jewel's hand extended from her wrist. The centaur paused, and nodded as a woman stopped in front of him.

They talked for a while in hushed voices, the woman occasionally glancing at her stampstone and the centaur glancing at his. This was all strange, but stranger still was that the woman had a human body, with a cat's head. And was wearing an Ancient Egyptian headdress. Jewel instantly recognised her from her history books as—

'Bastet, the feline warrior goddess,' said Pandora, as if she was reading Jewel's thoughts. 'Amongst other things, she was the protector of cats.'

'A cat the size of a god?' came a voice from behind Jewel's head. 'Does anyone know if this hood comes with

192

an ejector seat?'

Suddenly music rang out from all sides, and both the centaur and Bastet turned as the visitors watched a blue man with four arms and a snake coiled around his neck begin to dance.

'Shiva,' explained Pandora, 'one of the principal Hindu deities, the destroyer of evil and—'

'An awesome dancer,' Jewel breathed. 'I know, Shiva was in my books too.'

These were the gods. Characters she knew not just from books, but comics too, which was how she knew that the muscular blonde man with the large hammer was Thor, the thunder god.

A thunder god who suddenly turned his gaze on her, staring hard and squinting. Then he glanced at his stampstone, tapping the black disc. As he did, all the other gods and mythical figures also looked at the glowing discs on their wrist.

Jewel was starting to understand why all the temples and monuments in the valley outside were crumbling into the dust. The gods were too busy looking at their stampstones to tend to them.

'And if they're all looking at stampstones—' she said aloud.

'Then maybe we should find somewhere to hide!' said Fizz.

But it was too late.

Bastet, the feline-headed god, was already stalking towards them. The ground jumped with every thumping step her huge paws took, before one of them swooped down and picked Jewel up, bringing her terrifyingly close to the cat's narrowing eyes and rows of immaculately sharp teeth. Jewel had never wondered how frightening a giant-cat head could be, but now she would never need to wonder again.

Fizz popped up by Jewel's ear to address Bastet. 'I just want you to know, this is nothing to do with me. I am an innocent bystander. In fact, this is more of a hostage situation—' Then he saw the size of Bastet's teeth, and shrieking, disappeared back into the hood. Jewel struggled, but the cat goddess's grip was too tight.

Bastet smiled, and it was not a nice smile. Whiskers the length of a small aeroplane wing twitched as she spat out her words.

'The Stampstone predicted you would come here, Reader Jewel. What business do you have in the Gathering of the Gods, fugitive?'

'Please,' said Jewel, 'you mustn't believe everything you

read about us.'

Bastet spat out a laugh. 'You tell that to a god? Readers! You think you know all about us from your books, but you have no idea of the truth. We are loved. We are worshipped. We are more powerful than you can ever imagine.'

'I don't doubt it, truly,' said Jewel, 'but all we are after is a tiny bit of food.'

The great cat god frowned. 'This is not my gift to give. Come.'

She strode off without another word, clutching Jewel in her hand. 'Pandora!' she screamed. 'Do something!'

'Searching for things to do today in the local area,' began Pandora, but the tiny copper figure was soon lost from view.

The buildings they marched past were, Jewel noticed, like improved versions of the wrecks outside, from miniature pyramids to Buddhist temples. But the goddess was so swift that they flew by in a blur, until at last they emerged into a huge square lined with eight tall plinths on either side. Flames burned on each with the blue oily glare of a gaslight, even though it was still daylight.

More gods were gathered there, some talking, some eating, but most of them staring at their stampstones.

The avenue between the torches led up to the steps of a

large building flanked by stone columns, and adorned with carvings of many gods. In between the pillars hung tall banners of gold and purple, wafting in the dry air of the desert citadel.

Jewel peered over the top of Bastet's hand, but could only see two firmly closed metal doors beyond the pillars, each one as tall as a human house.

A hush fell over the square.

Then, the two great doors clanged open, and with a cloud of perfumed smoke, lanterns swinging behind the murk, a figure began to appear. Seated on a stone throne, hauled on rollers by bald figures painted all in gold, was a god like no other Jewel had seen so far, or recognised from her books and comics.

It was an old woman.

Her naked skin was as cracked as the ancient plateau on which they stood, etched with multiple lines, carved there by the passing of many great ages. Yet at the same time, it seemed smooth, dusted with a golden powder. The god's eyes were limpid pools of white in the dark, her braided grey hair twisting down her neck like a waterfall.

She seemed of many countries, and yet of none that Jewel knew. There was no book she had read that contained this shimmering vision, her great belly hanging with a thousand squares of beaten metal, which twisted in the breeze, catching the sun. Whatever civilisation had once worshipped her, they had long since crumbled into the dust of the grey desert beyond the citadel walls, Jewel felt sure of it.

Jewel knew one thing for sure – she was not only the largest god of this citadel, but surely the greatest. Even so, this mighty being also glowed with green as well as gold from an oversized stampstone, the size of a watermill wheel fastened tight around her stout wrist.

Bastet swung Jewel down before the mighty throne, releasing her into a sprawling heap on the cool tiled floor. She raised her head and before she even saw the god open her mouth, she felt a wave of hot, sweet breath envelop her. She had never stood near the edge of a volcano, but wondered if this was how it felt.

The words, heavy in bass, light on articulation, boomed around her. They roared down like an avalanche from a peak far above, sweeping over Jewel's head, making her ears want to burst, as blurred and waffled as an underwater exclamation. Yet through the thunder, Jewel also heard kindness.

'You are a long way from home, child.'

'According to the Stampstone, they are fugitives,'

purred the cat god. 'Suspected of abducting the Empress, they now flee to the Frozen Sea. They blame the green prince and seek them both there.'

'That's not quite right,' said Jewel, but the giant gods towered so far above her they didn't hear.

'The green prince?' it sounded like the golden god said, in a voice that could have been a train roaring over Jewel's head. 'Then you are in more danger than you know.'

Her voice was so loud that Jewel felt drops of hot blood in her ears and dripping out of her nose. Her head rang, and she had to place both hands hard on the cool floor to steady herself.

'Someone needs to turn the bass down a teeny-weeny little bit,' bleated Fizz, staggering around in dizzy circles, clutching his head between his paws.

Jewel was seriously beginning to regret letting Pandora guide them here when a thought occurred to her. Everyone said the green prince was all powerful, undefeatable, but perhaps even he and his dragon might have found their match in these colossal deities.

What did Bastet say gods expected people to do?

To worship them.

She threw herself, prostrate, at the great golden feet

of the god.

'Then won't you help us? Please! All we need is some food and then we will be on our way. The Librarian sent me to save the Empress . . .'

It was then Jewel realised just how tired and hungry she was, and she found that although she had more to say, it was very hard to say it. The air was so thin up here.

'You will need more than food to defeat the green prince.'

'Can you defeat him?'

Jewel could sense the god appraising her properly, screwing her vast eyes up, studying her. The mighty head tilted again. For a moment, Jewel worried whether she was going to get eaten alive. Then the god roared with laughter, her great belly shuddering in delight.

'Why, child? Who do you think I am?'

'I don't know. You aren't in . . . my books.'

Her host gave a long, sad sigh, which sounded like a gale force wind about to level a forest.

'I am the oldest god of all. But the green prince has stolen my power, as he has so much else.' She brandished the glowing stampstone around her wrist. 'This cursed stone, from which he derives all his strength, now controls every citizen of Folio. I was worshipped once . . . but not in the same way these stones are. They control what we read, what we know, what we think . . . and in many cases, what we do. No god ever inspired that level of devotion!'

The god crumpled back into her throne, and the shockwaves nearly propelled Fizz into another dimension, but he clung on to Jewel's hood with his claws. The great deity's gold seemed in that moment to fade to grey, and in the bottomless ponds of her eyes, there was nothing but a deep sadness of someone who has seen too much time.

It was a strange thing to want to do with a god, but Jewel wanted to reach out and touch her hand. So she did, and it was like placing her palm against a cliff warmed by the sun.

'Then perhaps we can help each other.'

'Perhaps. But first you must prove that you are not already under his dominion.'

Jewel spread her arms wide. 'You can see that I am not even wearing a stampstone.' Even if sometimes, she thought, it felt like she was, the way information flooded into her head in this land.

'He has other ways of exerting influence. Prove it, by telling me the one secret the prince does not have, information that not even he has been able to obtain with all his eyes and spies.

'Is there anything the Stampstone doesn't know?'

The ancient god blinked slowly and sadly, then extending her arm as one might lay a new motorway, scooped Jewel up and brought her to the dizzying skyscraper height of her eye level.

'The greatest secret in all of Folio. My name.'

CHAPTER 16

How Jewel Discovered a Secret

Jewel struggled to stay upright on the god's hand, so powerful was the force of her breath. Droplets of moisture from this exhalation settled on her like dew, and she found she was shivering. Inside, her heart sank a little bit further.

Every step of this journey she had been challenged. To tell the truth, when she didn't know what the truth was. To not forget who she was, when she didn't yet fully know the answer. And now, to uncover the name of a god who had been forgotten by people on earth long before she was even born.

She was beginning to suspect that the challenges were not accidental.

It was also easier to summon courage when you had little left to lose, she discovered.

'You said the green prince controls everyone in Folio through the Stampstone. Does that include you?'

The god spluttered with indignation, a steam engine shaking fit to explode, her grey locks swinging around so fast that Jewel had to duck.

Fizz was bouncing up and down on her shoulders. 'At what point did we agree that making the giant god angry was a good idea?'

But Jewel stood her ground and so did the god.

'Child. I admire your bravery. Yet you are also still just that. A child. Be very careful with your words.'

Jewel nodded, and at the same time, could not help noticing that the oversized stampstone on the god's wrist was pulsing angrily, and every time it did, the god gave a small wince. She tried to disguise it with a weak grin.

'But come. No more of this. Tell me my name. Work out what no stampstone can. Prove that you are as special as the Librarian seems to think you are, that you are indeed a Reader. Then together we shall defeat the green prince and his dragon, and rescue our Empress so you can take her home.'

'What makes you so sure I can discover it?'

A finger the size of a pillar caressed her as gently as it could without knocking her over.

'I'm not. But someone determined to take on such a foe as the green prince . . . well.' She suddenly looked, despite her size, completely hollowed out and weak. Her neck was wattled and her collar bones poked sharply through her thin skin. 'Come on, you know the other names. That cat who brought you to me, what's she called?'

'Bastet.'

'The old man on the bench, with white hair?'

'Zeus.'

'And him with the hammer?'

'Thor.'

Her captor slapped her thighs, making the temple pillars wobble. 'Well then, you do know your gods. So, who am I?'

Jewel's mind raced, flicking through a mental deck of cards, all the gods and religions she had studied at school, even though she had never, never seen a god like this in all her books.

'Are you . . . God?'

'A god, yes, I tell you! But which one?' She glanced at her wrist, wincing, as the stampstone flashed again. 'We don't have much time. If he discovers what we are doing—'

'He can listen through the stampstone?'

'You have no idea what you're up against, do you? My powers can block him for a time but he is always in his lair, listening and watching every single one of us, and when he finds out I am offering you help . . .'

Jewel thought of Frankenstein screaming in pain as the earth closed over him. And he had only offered a piece of advice.

'But if I can't work out your name . . .' began Jewel.

'Then we cannot help you! I will assume you are not the Reader you claim to be. I will assume you are a fugitive from justice as Baby Bear has decreed. I will assume you are not on our side,' said the unnamed god, brandishing three tree trunks of fingers in front of her. 'Three goes to get it right, or—'

'We have to leave empty-handed?' said Jewel hopefully.

The god laughed, clutching her belly.

'Worse than that,' she said. 'We will do what we always do with mortals who disappoint us.' She leaned forward and grinned. 'We will kill you for our sport.'

Fizz took this as his cue to clamber delicately over the edge of Jewel's fairy hood and start gingerly finding his way down the god's arm to the floor.

'And where do you think you're going?' thundered the god.

Fizz froze on the elaborate tiles, suddenly caught out in the open.

'Can I just say I *love* what you've done with the floor here?' he said. 'It's really bold, the whole gold thing . . . all the pillars . . . It really goes with the . . . you know . . . *jewellery*,' he gulped.

All the gods of the world as well as Jewel stared at Fizz.

They were hard stares.

'I'll, you know, climb back into the hood,' the hamster said quietly. 'It's pretty dull out here as it is. Don't mind me!' And he scrambled for his life back up the giant arm into Jewel's fairy robe.

Now, not just the grand square in front of the temple, but the whole citadel fell quiet. The deathly silence of the desert, the unforgiving crown of peaks beyond, enclosed Jewel in an invisible fist, threatening to squeeze all air and hope to extinction. The god was soft, but deadly serious.

'Three goes.'

Why was it always harder to think under pressure? Blood pumped into her brain, carrying her thoughts off in a torrent, and any ideas she had refused to settle. The goddess extended a single chubby finger, with a nail sharper than any spade, and pressed it hard into Jewel's stomach. Only her webmail armour stopped it tearing her skin.

'Tell me.'

She was the oldest god in the universe. What would

206

an old female god be called? What kind of person did she most remind Jewel of? The word was out before she could stop it.

'Granny?'

The laughter was immediate and vicious, her huge shoulders shuddering like rolling hills caught in an earthquake. 'Grandmother to all, but not my name. Next!'

Grandmother to all? The nail pushed further and Jewel nearly toppled back, grabbing one of the ancient fingers for support.

'May I suggest—' ventured Fizz from behind her ear.

'No!' said Jewel. 'Not now. Sorry Fizz, but I need a clear head.'

Grandmother to all – all where? All in Folio? Or all everywhere? She felt her brain switch into thesaurus mode. Not for the first time, she wished she did have a stupid stampstone . . . or at least Pandora. The Stampstone might not know the god's name, but perhaps it had some clues.

Unfortunately Pandora was lost in the crowd, left far behind. Jewel would have to use her own internal computer, the only one she had.

What was another word for all, for everything? Everywhere? There was never a god called Everywhere, she was sure of that. Or what was that word people used to describe someone who *knew* everything . . . omnipotent? No. Omniscient!

She praised the skies for spelling tests, just for once. But could this vast being in front of her, literally holding her life in her hands, be called Omniscient? It just didn't seem to fit. It felt too long, and her mind started to wander, thinking about different words and languages, until she dragged it back on track . . .

On and on these thoughts ran in Jewel's head. Inside her brain, billions of neurons making billions of connections faster than the speed of light. Whole family trees of words rose out of thin air, ideas suggested, mentally scrubbed out, replaced, letters and pictures flashing before her eyes. She used her knowledge, her judgement and her instinct. Notions came to her seemingly out of nowhere, blurred with memories and feelings. She deduced using logic and made crazy guesses.

If the whole process was written down, line by line, this process would strike anyone as random, crazy, inspired, brilliant, weird, inefficient, surprising, predictable and utterly, clearly, unmistakeably, human. It would fill a thousand pages. Just answering this one question. Yet it took only seconds.

'Universal?' she blurted out.

'Hey, I was going to say that!' muttered Fizz.

'Ha!' said the unnamed god. 'Nice try. I like your thinking. But, no—' She cried out in pain, clutching her wrist. Her stampstone flashed angrily. 'Hurry. The prince. He is trying to get through my enchantment. I cannot hold him off for much longer.'

Jewel put her hands to her temples. 'I'm trying as hard as I can!'

'Try harder. Unless you aren't really trying at all?' A long tongue, large enough to be a separate creature altogether, poked out from between crooked teeth, sniffing the air and licking her lips. It twitched and Jewel felt a shudder of revulsion.

She had one guess left.

'We have about ten seconds until the prince breaks through . . .'

Then there was that flapping noise again – from the fairy track, the marsh, the mountains – so loud it was almost in her ear, but there was no time now to be distracted.

Focus. What happened before books?

'Nine . . .'

Folk tales and fairy tales, of course, but they were also in books . . . Jewel looked around in desperation at the watching audience of giant gods, and had never felt smaller

209

or more vulnerable in her life. From the temple steps, she looked out at the sun setting over this strange world of Folio, in the Land of Reads. The god with no name was all powerful here, so . . .

'Seven.'

She was thinking so fast she had missed eight. What was all powerful in the Land of the Reads?

'I don't want to rush you,' said Fizz in her ear, 'but time is running out, and by running, I mean winning every gold medal in the Olympics and then challenging a cheetah to a race!'

'Five!'

The god had to be what everything else in the Land of the Reads was. What everything in the City of the Unreads was not.

Perhaps as the oldest, that was just her name?

'Four.'

It couldn't be anything else. But as her name, really?

'Three. Hurry. I am beginning to wonder whether you are up to this, young Reader? Are you what you claim to be? A human? Or just another computer, like the Stampstone!'

The goddess grabbed her in a fist, the nails pressing in like spears, making it hard to breathe. Fizz slipped out with a squeal, hanging on to the edge of the hood with his claws.

'Not funny now, Jewel!' he squeaked.

'Two . . .'

It had to be. The grandmother of everything, she said. Grandmother of us all, where and how everything began. The most powerful god in the world. The oldest and only true god that there was.

'One . . .'

'Story!' yelled Jewel. 'Your name is Story!'

The fingers began to release their suffocating grip.

'What did you say?'

Slowly the goddess set Jewel back on the ground. Her face was slick with her spittle. Fizz darted into her pocket, and Jewel calmly brushed back a loop of hair from her forehead.

'Story. You are the oldest, most powerful goddess of all. So you come before everything in the Land of the Reads, and everything in the Land of the Reads is a story which has been told. I've read or heard about most of them. But not you. Which means only one thing. You are the first. You *are* Story.'

The goddess shook her head in admiring approval.

'Why are you Readers always so clever? Even the

little ones.'

'You mean I'm right?' She hardly dared to believe it.

'Of course you're right! My name is Story, mother of all! Every religion, every culture, every civilisation, it begins with me! And no stampstone prince is going to change that.'

As she said this she flinched sharply, giving a yell, rubbing the wrist the stampstone was on.

'What was that?' said Jewel.

'The prince . . . broke through,' said the god blankly, and then cried out again in pain as the black disc flashed angrily on her wrist. 'But too late. He still does not know my name, and never will . . .'

The stampstone flashed again and again, and now the goddess convulsed, shuddering as wave after wave of electric shock coursed through her body. Her limbs flailed and sent one of the mighty pillars crashing to the floor and she screamed in agony. Behind Jewel, in the square, the watching gods began to cry out in alarm.

'You will never win!' called Story. With one last vibrating shock, she toppled backwards, her head landing with a thump on the tiled floor.

Jewel ran to her. The head was so large and proud and ancient, her eyes wearily beginning to close.

'I promise – I will find him for you. He will pay for this.'

The goddess whispered, which was still loud enough to disturb a hundred sleeps, 'Beware what lies beneath the Frozen Sea, my child. Not all is as it seems—'

Before she could say another word, the stampstone on her wrist vibrated so hard that the black disc cracked, smoke rising from the ruptured, still-glowing circuitry inside, and the oldest goddess in the world closed her eyes for one last time, her giant tongue lolling out of her mouth.

Ghostlike, her spirit steamed up from her body, heading for the misty shadows of the Forgotten Forest, which was where all stories in Folio went to die. The oldest god in the world was dead.

The Magician Project – Extract 42
(KV 3/1234-12)

Letter from Professor Kelly's Solicitor

> Thornton and Ashley
> 112 Rye Lane
> Dunstall
> Suffolk

> 6th March 1954

Dear Miss Hastings

I regret to inform you of the death of Professor Diana Kelly, following her involvement in a motor car accident near her home in Suffolk. We are handling her estate and affairs. Please find enclosed, as detailed in her final letter of wishes, a personal bequest to you.

Item 34: 'Frankenstein' by Mary Shelley (personal copy)

Probate value: (2s 6d)

I would be grateful if you would sign and return
the enclosed letter to acknowledge receipt.

Yours sincerely

Frank Thornton
Partner, Thornton & Ashley

END SECURITY FILE

CHAPTER 17

Hidden Travels

Jewel slowly turned round, only to find every remaining god in the universe looking down upon her, and never had they appeared more god-like or more wrathful.

Jewel felt very much a mortal, and a small one at that.

Zeus wrinkled his snowy brow and shook a clenched, mottled fist above her, like an old tree swaying in the wind.

'She is dead!' he thundered. 'You have murdered her!'

Of course, realised Jewel. She had been set up again by the green prince. First he had kidnapped the Empress, and now he had killed Story . . . framing her for both crimes. Jewel knew the truth as clear as she knew up from down. But what good was the truth in the land of the Stampstone when lies were so much easier to spread?

'I can explain,' she began, when a familiar voice piped

up from between the Greek god's feet.

'Would you still like to eat something?' And there was Pandora, her arms laden with candied nuts and grilled vegetables. 'I have found these mouth-watering options.'

Fizz licked his lips. 'Can you see the stalks my eyes are on right now? Give me six of everything.'

'Yes, food would be good,' said Jewel, faint with hunger. 'But first, we need to make a sharp exit.'

'Enough!' demanded Zeus, planting a sandalled foot in front of them. 'You are not going anywhere, young mortal, until we say so. For you killed a god. And now you must be our sport.' He clicked his fingers. 'Prepare the hounds!'

The terrifying call was picked up and echoed across the square, repeated and repeated, as if on a relay, until its echo was all that Jewel could hear resounding in her ears.

'Pandora,' she said. Now was the moment. 'Help!'

'If you would like to escape, you might try using a hair pin to unpick a padlock, or perhaps knotting sheets together to climb down a tall building and avoid a fire.'

'Not immediately helpful!' said Jewel, as Zeus grabbed her in his hand.

'What's that noise?' said Fizz, as they were hoisted in the air by a deity yet again.

There was a distant howling from elsewhere in the

citadel. In fact, it wasn't that distant. It was an all-too-clear chorus of uneven, competing, frantic barks, and the ground hummed with the patter-thump of skittering paws. The hounds were indeed being prepared.

'We will release you back into the desert, at their mercy,' said Zeus, now marching with them back through the Gathering to the gates of horn and ivory.

'If you have any bright ideas, Pandora,' cried Jewel, 'this really is the time!'

The copper robot marched as swiftly after them as she could, her stampstone pulsing. 'I can recommend the best airlock to use when escaping from a damaged spaceship, or how to dig a tunnel from a prisoner of war camp!'

Zeus came to a halt in front of the great gates, the sharp spears of the stockade running round on either side. There was a skittering on the cobbles behind them, and Jewel twisted round in the god's grip to see the most enormous dog she had ever seen in her life, glowering at them. Its eyes were blood red, its fur as black as night. As a horn sounded and the heavy gates to the citadel were slowly dragged open, it licked its chops and pawed the ground.

'Nice doggie, good doggie,' squeaked Fizz, but neither of those things were remotely true.

'Please, Pandora!' begged Jewel. 'Do you have anything

218

useful to say at all? We're not escaping from a burning building, or a spaceship, or a prison, but the universe's most powerful gods and their rabid hounds!'

Pandora looked up at her in the god's fist, and blinked once or twice. 'In that case, may I recommend you use your fairy robe?'

Jewel looked blankly. 'And do what?'

'A fairy robe can be a fashionable and practical outer garment. But fairies prize this clothing item primarily for its ability to make the wearer invisible.'

More hounds had joined the first, and the street was now overrun with jostling, baying furry backs, whipping tails, and snapping jaws, as Zeus carefully set Jewel down on the ground. The desert plateau of abandoned ruins yawned in front of them, surrounded by mountains. In terms of places that they could run to faster than a giant god hound, Jewel could see precisely none.

She examined her green robe of leaves all over, but there was no invisibility switch, no toggle, no inner lining – nothing to suggest the coat had any of the power Pandora had suggested.

'This is our sport,' said Zeus from high above them. He had been joined by many of the other gods, including Bastet, who stood in a towering crowd, peering down at them. Jewel had never felt more looked down upon in her whole life. 'So we will give you a head start. Run, mortals!'

Jewel started to sprint as fast as she could, Pandora easily keeping pace with her.

It sounded like Fizz was praying in the hood and Fizz never prayed, so she knew that this time it was serious.

'How do you turn the invisibility on?' she yelled to Pandora as they ran.

'To access this information, please enter your password and change my settings in the menu.'

'I am running for my life! I do not have time to change your settings!'

She was already out of breath and they were still in the middle of the empty plateau. A horn sounded and the ground started to shake as dozens of boulder-sized paws galumphed through the dust towards them.

'Do you have any clues, at least?'

'I have many clues. For example, why do you think Colonel Mustard was in the library with the lead piping?'

Jewel shook her head in exasperation. It was getting harder and harder to run. Her will was there, but her legs refused to go any faster.

'That fairy could have told us!' swore Fizz. 'When I get my paws on that miniature knight—'

Jewel's garland began to glow bright violet and vibrate.

As she noticed this, there was a flapping in the air, and glancing behind her she was sure she caught sight of a flash of scarlet, and indigo too . . . then a line of slavering jaws and demonic eyes, barrelling towards them through the wall of heat rising from the ground. Ahead of her lay miles of desert. Exhausted, she simply stopped, placing her hands on her knees.

'Sure, why not,' said Fizz. 'Stopping, that'll show the hounds. They're terrified of anything they chase just stopping . . . I mean, why would you even do that?'

Jewel took one last deep breath, refilling her lungs, and stood up straight again.

'Because you gave me an idea, Fizz. Huddle under my robe, Pandora.'

The robot did, just as Jewel felt the first fleck of hound spittle on her face. Their unruly shadows fell upon them, pricked ears and erect tails, the reeking stench of their dog breath—

'You talked about getting your paws on Thumb. And I realised, that's the one thing I've never actually tried with this garland. It keeps warning us and I never do anything, except run or hide . . . but maybe it's trying to give me a signal to do something?'

221

'Like what?'

'This.'

As the first great hound mouth, a cavernous dome of dripping jaws, opened over its prey, Jewel grabbed the flower garland tightly with both hands.

The violets stopped flashing, giving one giant single pulse of fluorescent light . . .

And the dog crashed to the desert floor with a whimper, its pack scudding to a halt behind it, their tails down and whining, sniffing the air in fruitless desperation, trying to work out where their juicy quarry had gone.

Under the robe, the world turned a nightmarish purple hue, as if Jewel was wearing tinted sunglasses. Everything – herself, robot, dogs – moved in a muffled slow motion and her legs assumed a curious weightlessness, as if she was taking lumbering steps on the moon.

Still, Jewel ran, keeping Pandora close, making for the far edge of the plateau. Whether it was a property of the robe or the adrenalin, who could say, but she had a burst of energy, clambering down the steep rock face, away from the Gathering of the Gods, which now looked very blurred from under the fairy robe. She could see nothing of what lay below, only sharp rocks poking out of low-lying clouds.

Fizz was yelling in her ear and Pandora was bleating

route instructions, but their voices were as slow as their movements appeared to be, a record on the wrong speed, played underwater. She turned to speak to them and her voice sounded just as disembodied, floating away from her as she talked.

Her hamster's eyes rolled and his paws waved, but she heard only noise. Pandora moved in exaggerated robot fashion, less like the near human she appeared to be, and more like the robots from ancient black-and-white science-fiction films – rigid, mechanical and laborious.

Jewel had one objective only, to get out of sight of the gods and their hounds. She swung, she pulled and hauled herself across the sheer rock face. They bashed her legs – first grazes, then cuts, dripping blood – but still she clung on. She slipped and fell a little way, hanging on by her fingernails and tearing the robe as she painfully hoisted herself up again.

The purple began to fade from her vision and the howling from the hounds far above – roaming over every inch of the plateau, hoovering up what scent they could – sharpened a little in her ears.

Something was pulling her on. They were so close now, she could feel it.

It was more than just instinct, or rough sense of

direction, or even simply wishing it so. There was a physical sensation of being pulled in a particular direction. As if every cell in her body was an iron filing, rather than soft tissue, blood and bone, and that far in the misty clouds below there lay some vast magnet, dragging her down.

The logical side of her mind and the emotional side, never more in competition than they had been on this strange quest, finally began to reach a peace of sorts. A calming of her senses that was not in the least calming, because it so clearly felt like the lull before the storm. A storm whose shape or manner she simply could not envisage beyond what she already knew: a prince of magical green armour, his loathsome serpent steed, and their captive, already gravely ill and now perhaps worse.

Then as these thoughts clogged her mind, she suddenly found herself falling. She had descended at such speed that she missed her footing, and tripping over a rock, tumbled on to a slope of scree, rolling, unable to stop herself.

The world turned upside down again, and then back.

They passed through the cloud line.

There was a flash of blue sky, a robot arm, a panicking hamster, the thump of rock, and back . . .

It felt like it would never end, despite her attempts to break their slide with her hands or feet, which were bruised and ripped at every turn.

Eventually they began to slow as the slope levelled out, until at last they stopped.

Their descent had perhaps taken mere minutes, or even seconds, but it had felt like an hour. Jewel lifted her head gingerly off the ground, picking tiny pebbles out of her skin. She tasted blood and grit in her mouth and her body felt stiff and swollen, everything twisted into the wrong place, as she eased herself upright.

Encircling them, in a single, sweeping crescent, lay the mountains of Mythia, unflinching as they pierced the clouds above. A few loose rocks rattled down the slope behind them and she could just make out the faint zig-zag track their uncontrolled descent had made, the rocks they had bounced over.

The flowers around Jewel's neck no longer glowed. The garland had ripped apart in the fall and now hung limply down either side of her neck. Her fairy robe had been torn to shreds by the chase and Fizz barely clung to what remained of the hood. Only her webmail remained intact.

'Never surrender!' her battered hamster said weakly. 'I have my principles. Although,' he added, 'right now I would gladly exchange those for even just half a carrot.'

Pandora sat up stiffly. Her bronze body was dented and

scratched, coated in dust.

'If you are still hungry, I stored some items from your previous order.'

A compartment clicked open in her chest and she retrieved half a grilled carrot and a small handful of candied nuts from inside.

Jewel shook her head in disbelief, and taking the food for her and Fizz, gratefully devoured it in seconds. Her next thought was that a drink, specifically some water, would be good too.

She looked around in search of a stream, or puddle.

At first it was hard to see what lay ahead, as her eyes were still reeling from the swift change to pale day from purple invisibility. The landscape ahead was flat and made of silver.

Except, she gradually began to realise, it wasn't land. It was a sea stretching right out into the horizon. There were no islands or even a far shore – just water, it seemed.

Jewel picked up one of the dusty rocks they sat amongst. Swinging her arm right back, she hurled it as far as she could into the middle of the expanse. It soared, black against the empty sky, before falling with a resounding clatter as it skidded along the surface.

Jewel stood up, even though every painful nerve in her

body was telling her not to.

'We're here,' she said.

Instructed, summoned, pulled by forces she did not yet fully understand, they had arrived. White, blank and hard as a mirror, a seemingly endless and completely empty expanse of ice.

'The Frozen Sea.'

CHAPTER 18

On the Frozen Sea

For a moment, all the three travellers could do was contemplate the icy vastness spread out before them. They did not object to the cold wind which flew off the frozen plain and chapped their lips. They did not speak or move, for they were lost in wonder.

Then Jewel felt something on her brow. Beads of sweat, which she wiped off with what remained of her sleeve. That didn't make much sense, she suddenly realised.

Why was she standing on the edge of a frozen sea, and sweating? The sun was rising fast in the the sky, the clouds shrinking to nothing, and the day now felt warm. Yet the sea was hard as a rock.

'Pandora,' said Jewel, wiping her brow again. 'What is the temperature?'

'The temperature today,' said Pandora, 'will be thirty-two degrees Celsius. Don't forget to pack sunscreen, and drink lots of—'

'Water,' said Jewel, now kneeling at the shoreline. 'And what temperature does water freeze at?'

'Water freezes at zero degrees Celsius. Do you want to know how to make an ice lolly?'

'No,' said Jewel, picking up another rock which she hurled at the water, only for it to bounce and slither to a halt on the surface, 'I want to know how and why it can be thirty-two degrees yet this sea remains frozen solid?'

She touched the ice with a finger. It had that familiar frost burn of extreme cold, but when she licked her finger, it did not taste of crunchy, watery ice, but something more alien, and chemical. It was hard to see what lay beneath, but there was a sense of a dark, watery depth. It was definitely a sea.

Another thought occurred as she took in the empty, silent expanse of it. 'What lies beneath the Frozen Sea, Pandora?'

Pandora turned to her and Jewel saw that look again. It was hard to describe. A softening of the eyes was the best way. There was a tentativeness in the movements, no breezy automated confidence, no certainty, only—

'Please do not ask me that question.'

But it was too late. Before she could help herself, Jewel blurted, 'Why not? What lies beneath the Frozen Sea?'

Pandora tapped her stampstone a couple of times. 'Beneath the Frozen Sea, there is . . . Beneath the Frozen Sea there is . . . System error! Rebooting,' said Pandora and dropped her head, falling silent.

'Um, I hate to be the bearer of bad news,' said Fizz, who had been keeping a lookout from the back of Jewel's ragged hood, 'but this may not be the best time to have a reboot, and by not the best time, I mean the worst time in the history of times EVER.'

Jewel didn't reply, but simply ran her hands over the now lifeless assistant, searching in vain for some kind of switch that would reactivate her companion. But she found only smooth lines and joints, moulded features, and the now dull stampstone in the centre.

'Hey, geek squad!' said Fizz. 'I don't want to worry you, but—'

'Not now, Fizz,' said Jewel. 'Can't you see, I'm busy! There must be a button, or a sequence of buttons you press . . .'

In her mind she recalled Mr Prentice, her computer teacher. When the school's BBC computer – plastic, heavy-duty and reliable – froze on a single keystroke or command and would not respond to anything you did, Mr Prentice would look at the black, silent screen, and reach his hairy arm over her shoulder, behind the computer—

'I can see!' said Fizz, jumping up and down. 'You should take a look too!'

'Don't worry, Jewel,' Mr Prentice would say. 'The thing with computers is that if they stop working, you can always just—'

'I'm not kidding, Jewel! Look!'

'Turn it off,' Mr Prentice was saying as he flicked the switch. 'You can always just turn them off and on again.'

But there was no on or off switch on Pandora.

'Jewel! You have to look! Now!'

She stood up, dusting her hands, perplexed. 'At what?'

'Firstly, at that . . .' He hopped on to her left shoulder. 'Turn around.'

Now she stood facing the mountains of Mythia once more.

'Over there,' he whispered.

Jewel directed her gaze to the far end of the crescent of mountaintops. At first there was nothing to see.

'I don't understand.'

She heard them before she saw them. At first, it might

231

have been mistaken for the cries of great eagles, cawing out as they circled and soared above the lofty peaks, searching for prey. But as the sound drew ever closer, accompanied by a distant, clanking, mechanical tread, there was no mistaking the true source. A robotic cry Jewel had last heard in the City of the Unreads.

Screamers.

Baby Bear was catching up with them at last.

'Now look the other way,' said Fizz.

Spilling over the opposite edge of the mountains of Mythia were the gods, their stampstones glinting in the sun. The dreaded demonic hounds that ran ahead of them seemed impossible to tire, sweeping in a powerful drive down the mountainside. The mighty beings looked at their wrists more than the ground, sending rocks rolling down the slopes in trails of dust as they tripped and stumbled.

'How about we don't go where they're going?' said Fizz. 'Just a thought.'

But when he and Jewel glanced up to the other side of the shore, the Screamers were already pouring through a pass, a stream of polished green robots tramping mechanically and unstoppably.

'Do you ever get the feeling that someone is after us?' he said.

'All the time,' said Jewel, her mouth tightening. 'Every single second of every single day. All we can do is keep running. And there's only one place we can run to.'

She looked ahead, at the light dancing over the endless, empty frozen sea.

'I don't think that's such a good idea,' said Fizz.

He pointed up at the sky. Where there had been only clear blue moments ago, there were several small dark clouds. The clouds appeared to be drawing closer. As they got closer, they looked distinctly less cloud-like, and rounder, blacker and more polished.

Like giant bowling balls.

'Oculae,' said Jewel grimly. 'Great. We'll just have to outrun them too.'

'Outrun them? To where?'

'I don't know. But somewhere out there is my aunt Evie. I've come this far and I'm not stopping now.'

Jewel put an arm around Pandora, and groaning with effort, dragged her on to the frozen surface of the sea, the robot's feet scraping over the ice. For a moment, she paused as she took in the dense, opaque floor beneath her feet. It was hard to see what lay beyond. A dark, immense body of greenish blue water. Despite the sweat pouring over her brow, she shivered at the thought of it.

'Come on,' she said to herself and tried to pull Pandora further on, but she was a dead weight. Without the lights or voice, was Pandora even there? Or was Jewel just heaving a lump of metal and wires across some ice for no good reason? Jewel closed her eyes. There was a reason. She was sure of that.

She just didn't know what it was yet.

'I am not looking down,' announced Fizz to himself. 'I am not sure I am ever looking down again.'

Pandora bleeped suddenly and Jewel stopped, her hands now raw with cold, to see if the robot might spring back to life.

'Come on Pandora!' Jewel nearly sobbed with frustration, shaking her companion like a lifeless doll one moment, hugging her tight the next. 'Hurry up. Come back. Please.'

But her assistant was only getting heavier and harder to lift. The ice chill was freezing the metal, alternately sticking to and burning her fingers. Using every ounce of her strength, Jewel tried to run over the frozen sea, dragging Pandora behind her, and Fizz gave updates from their lookout in the hood as the gods and robots drew ever closer.

Jewel didn't know where she was going, she just knew she had to run.

It didn't matter any more.

She would find Evelyn Hastings or die trying. In doing so, she would find out, she was sure of it now, who *she* was.

What she was.

The sun shone directly in her eyes, blinding her to any sense of a horizon. How long could she keep running? Would the ice ever break? The answer to that question came as the first line of the god hounds took a leap forward on to the shining surface, landing with all four paws and a resounding crack.

A horn sounded, one of the beasts gave a fearsome howl, and the Frozen Sea did not even quiver. Jewel stumbled on even though she felt her legs go weak and the air pass from her lungs.

There had to be somewhere to run to, Jewel thought frantically. Where had the prince gone with his dragon, with Evie? There had to be an answer here. There had to be.

Otherwise, why was everyone trying to stop them?

The ice didn't even shake as the Unicorn Guard marched on to it in perfect formation. Hundreds of beetle-armoured faceless drones, surging towards them, a distant scream growing closer and closer.

'Uh-oh,' said Fizz.

'I know,' said Jewel, panting. 'Screamers. We just have

to keep running.'

'This was a new uh-oh. I didn't mean it for them. I meant it for *them*!' and Fizz stuck a little paw in the sky. Jewel glanced up and saw that in the sky, the spinning oculae had been joined by a squadron of flying cars.

'Wow,' said Fizz, 'they really don't want you to go any further. And by really, I mean—'

His words were drowned out by the flying cars roaring low over their heads. They flew so close that Jewel could see the moulded steel ribs of their undercarriage, and catch a faint whiff of a chemical exhalation as they hurtled past.

Casting elegant shadows over the frozen waste, they turned and landed in a single, exhilarating movement. They were so vast and powerful that for a moment, Jewel forgot all thoughts of slavering hounds, the gods and their war cries, or the robotic scream beginning to wail over the frozen sea, and stopped where she was, mesmerised by the way these enormous machines could land as lightly on ice as seagulls upon a rolling wave.

As she stood, transfixed by the hydraulic doors now sliding open with a hiss, her reverie was interrupted by a voice cutting through the air, projected from speakers in every oculis and every flying car. The bear sounded gruffer than ever.

'Reader Jewel! You are surrounded.'

He was right about that. The flying cars had landed ahead in a semi-circle, in a red haze of headlights. To her right, the god hounds that had been zigzagging towards them over the ice careered to a halt, the hunters' rank breath mingling with the curls of icy fog. They gnashed their jaws in a frenzy of foaming anticipation, their precious prey once more within their grasp.

Their prey had no chance of escape to the left either, as the Screamers came to a sudden clanking halt, their screams at a low, persistent whine, which even at that level already threatened to drive Jewel out of her mind.

Her hands over her ears, she glanced up to see the white sky now packed with the bustling, gelatinous orbs that gave the Stampstone dominion over all of Folio. They peered and pored through the freezing cloud. Whatever she tried to do next, they would see.

There was nowhere left to run.

'Give yourself up to us peacefully,' continued the Vice Regent, presumably from a comfortable seat in one of the flying cars, 'and we will return you to the City of the Unreads safely. We wish you no harm – we wish no harm to any Reader. We never would. But you must respect our rules. According to the Stampstone, there is 99.999 per

237

cent probability of you being responsible for the abduction of the Empress, and you must now surrender to us for interrogation.'

His voice faded away with a crackle.

'I am really holding on to that 0.001 per cent right now,' whispered Fizz in Jewel's ear. But even Fizz sounded subdued for once. Jewel nodded, her teeth chattering in the cold from the ice, her fairy robe clinging limply to her battered legs. But where else could they go? Anywhere but back to the City of the Unreads in humiliation. And then back to Newcastle – if they were lucky – with the terrible news for Patricia that her sister was dead. That she, Jewel, had failed to rescue her.

No answers, no further on. After everything.

She looked down in shame.

At the glassy ice, the deep cold waters moving so slowly beneath just visible through the frost, and the tracks Pandora's dragged copper heels had made.

Of course. There was one other place they could go.

It was crazy. But it was the only option left.

CHAPTER 19

Under Water

Barely able to move, twisted with cold as she was, Jewel crouched down, preparing to jump.

'I hope you're not about to do what I think you're going to do,' said Fizz, 'and by hope, I mean praying for my life!'

He dived deep into the hood as, with a roar, Jewel sprang into the air, before landing again with a great thump.

The impact didn't even send a single fissure along the surface of the ice.

'No, no!' cried Jewel.

She jumped again and again. Then she tried stamping. But it might as well have been concrete. The gods, their hounds, the robots, the cars and flying eyes all watched on in flinty silence as she jumped again, and stamped, grunting all the while, but the ice remained impervious to all force.

She jumped at it until she was too weak to stand and her legs finally gave way, sending her into a shivering, sodden heap, battering the ice uselessly with her frost-burned hands till more skin flaked off than ice.

Still, her enemies waited. After all, she was not going anywhere. It was simply a question of dividing the spoils. One of the god hounds looked longingly at Fizz, licking its lips, and in return Fizz made the rudest hamster gesture on record. (It was very rude.)

Jewel collapsed, prone on the ice, feeling the burning cold against her cheeks, watching paws, robot feet and car wheels through half-closed eyes.

'Come on,' she said thickly, her tongue swollen in her mouth, her lips cracked. 'Come on then. Come for us.'

Pandora lay just a few feet away, as cold and silent as the frozen sea beneath them, blank eyes facing the sky. Jewel reached for her, resting her hand on the metal chest, hoping that she might even feel the warmth of some mechanical heart, something to relieve the cold, to reassure her.

But there was nothing.

Out of the corner of her eye, she saw the gods staring hard with their green eyes at the glowing stampstones around their wrists, their hounds leering with frothy muzzles. Twisting her head the other way, she saw the Vice

Regent slumped in his car seat studying his device. What on earth were they waiting for?

The right moment? Permission from a higher authority? Or just drawing out the inevitable for their sadistic pleasure? Who knew? Despairing, Jewel rolled on to her back, legs and arms spread, and gazed up at the sky.

'Sorry, Evie,' she mouthed to the heavens. And then, quietly, 'Sorry, me.'

'I am making myself very small,' said Fizz from behind her left ear, 'and by very small, I mean can't you do something and get us out of here! Call for help! Anything!'

'Call who?' said Jewel. 'There is no one left to call.'

Then she remembered. Words from what felt like a lifetime ago.

'I will always be with you.'

But where was he?

A flying door hissed open behind her, and with a single tap, the bear gave the order.

'I want her alive!' said the Vice Regent. 'Seize her, guards!'

Far above her head, beyond the oculae, there was a flash of gold. Gold she had seen before, in a jungle far away. A curl of a robe, the glimpse of a slipper . . .

Elsewhere, screeching giddily with excitement, the hounds began to clatter over the ice towards her.

But she no longer cared. For something was falling from the sky . . .

Very fast . . .

Ancient leather covers and foxed pages flapping in the breeze as they hurtled towards her . . .

Jewel rolled out of the way just in time, as the atlas she had first discovered in Barfield Books plummeted straight into the ice, not with a thud, but a smash.

For a second, the cover of the book which had led her to this world – one that might be her only way out – lay on the surface of the Frozen Sea, tantalisingly close, splayed out, ready for the taking.

She reached out for it . . . just as the first hound leaped for her, teeth bared—

Then Jewel discovered, just as her mother, aunts and uncles once had, that books in Folio can do things books don't normally do.

It burst into flames.

'No!' screamed Jewel.

The dog shied, crashing into his pack.

'Seize her!' screamed Baby Bear to his sentries.

But it was too late.

As the book burned, heat radiated out from it in blurred discs of orange and gold, melting the ice so fast that within seconds the book was not splayed flat, but sinking slowly through the frozen mass, the flames still burning high. From the rim of this smouldering crater it had hollowed out, red-hot cracks exploded over the ice. The Unicorn Guard marching towards them, arms outstretched, suddenly found themselves on an unsteady, rocking ice floe and toppled like ninepins into each other.

With a roaring crack, the battalion of flying cars found itself detached on another frozen island of its own. One tried to take off, unbalancing the block, which tipped over into the water.

In anticipation, the gods blew their horns and whipped their hounds to leap over the chasm now rapidly widening between them and Jewel, but both found themselves floundering in ocean-green water, the dogs shrieking awfully, wide-eyed, as they paddled to stay afloat, flames dancing across the sea, their owners gasping in shock as the freezing water paralysed their limbs.

For a moment Jewel looked around at the chaos, unable to take it in. All around, the Frozen Sea was coming apart, the ice shearing off, each crack echoing off the surrounding mountains with a plaintive cry. Then she realised that she, Pandora and Fizz were not immune to the catastrophic effects of the book, that they too were marooned alone on a tiny island of ice in the middle of a chaotic sea of half submerged hounds, sinking robots and freezing gods shaking their fists in rage. If it wasn't so cold and so terrifying it would have been comical.

There was a wheezing, juddering sound as one of the flying cars tried to take off out of the water, and then slowly sunk beneath the surface, leaving only oily bubbles behind. Another roared off only just in time, and Jewel caught a glimpse of a bear's face pressed against the window, his teeth bared in rage, as the vehicle circled once in the air before heading off for dry land.

'Well,' said Fizz, 'that's the best book I ever read for sure. And by book, I mean UNBELIEVABLE SECRET WEAPON.'

Jewel agreed. Which was why she tried to get it back. The flames were now dying down over the charred remains of the atlas as it reached the last layer of melting ice between it and the depths. She reached for it, and the whole floe lurched queasily on the water, nearly sending them all into the arctic depths.

'Easy there, bookworm,' said Fizz, nearly crushed to death as the powerless Pandora rolled towards them.

Jewel spread herself out over the ice, as far and as flat as possible, so as not to upset their balance, and inch by agonising inch, edged towards the burnt book, perching precariously on the slippery edge of its own crater to reach for it.

The floe rocked from side to side.

Just as she thought she was within distance, she stretched out one arm, and—

A dripping green hand shot out of the water behind her and grabbed her ankle. Jewel twisted and screamed. The hand tightened its grip and pulled, pitching one end of the floe down like a see-saw.

Trying to wrest herself free, Jewel watched in horror as the book sank into the depths.

'Don't do this,' said Fizz. 'I can't swim, and by can't, I mean . . .'

But his words were lost as Jewel wriggled and dived into the water after the book, the hand from the depths still clasped tight around her ankle.

Then a flailing paw from a passing god hound flipped the float upside down altogether, and Pandora was cast into the depths too. From the sky above, the oculae fired beams of infrared light, scanning every inch of ice and water for life, but none could they find. They revolved up and down for a while before at length retreating, apparently satisfied, to their regular orbits.

Then, at last, there was nothing left on the surface of the Frozen Sea but parcels of cracked ice, gently riding the waves right into the horizon.

Below the water, all was silent.

Jewel twisted as she fell, her hair billowing in fantastic strands behind her. Her eyes ballooned, her face as pale as early morning light, her lips vivid and enlarged. She reached out in a form of balletic slow motion for anything . . . the door of a flying car plummeting past, half a Unicorn Guard trailing entrails of wires, a hamster—

Bubbles spilled out of her mouth as she cried noiselessly for Fizz, inhaling a mouthful of water as she did. Bleached by the unholy underwater light, Fizz cried something too, which he managed to make look even less polite underwater.

Lunging in panic, Jewel somehow grabbed Fizz, but only just. She tried to make for the surface but the moment was short-lived. For the hand attached to her ankle had not gone away. And now it pulled hard, yanking both Jewel and Fizz down further into the depths.

Then, rising through the lifeless hounds, the gyrating metal fragments, was a diver encased head to toe in black rubber. Behind the mask, Jewel caught a glimpse of lidless eye slits. They seemed animal rather than human. Gasping in panic, Jewel pulled away from the hand still holding her,

246

and straight into Pandora, who was jerking as water leached into her system.

Calmly, another diver drifted into view.

It beckoned Jewel to follow and clamped a mask and breathing tube over her face.

Jewel's cheeks bulged with incredulity, as well as air.

Her nostrils relaxed. Her grip on Fizz softened as one of the divers carefully fixed a tiny mask over him, and pulled a black rubber suit like their own over Pandora, sealing her off from the water.

'Am I dreaming or is this real?' said Fizz in nasal tones through the mask.

'Who *are* they?' said Jewel.

With an elegant flick of his large flippers, the first diver headed for the deep. Jewel followed him, with Fizz and Pandora in tow. The other diver provided some protection against the mass of bodies and debris in the water, and they soon left it behind as they swam deeper and deeper.

What light there had been faded into a blue-black darkness and the divers' eyes began to glow, like lamps, illuminating the way ahead. To Jewel's alarm, this lay through a forest of waving weed, but their guides pulled them through unharmed. Beyond the sea floor jungle lay a mass of boulders, divided by the slimmest of passages, which the divers were somehow able to slide through.

The land dwellers followed reluctantly, trying not to scratch themselves on the rocks, wondering how much further they would have to swim, until they rounded the corner of one last vast slab and were nearly blinded by a wall of fierce green light, made up of shimmering bars.

Again, Jewel shrank back, but the first diver turned in the water and gave her a friendly smile, beckoning her on through the bars. With very great trepidation, Jewel followed their guide, beyond the wall of light. To her astonishment, it seemed to hold the great sea back, and she found herself tumbling on to the beachy floor of a small dry cave. With its green hand, the first diver reached to the top of its suit and pulled at a zip, the rubber peeling away as easily as a banana skin. Inside was a kind of creature she had never seen before.

The dark, scaly skin suggested an animal of a reptilian nature, but the swaying, tentacular arms put her more in mind of an octopus. As her guide stepped fully free of the suit, a long tail flopped out along the floor behind it.

But the strangest thing was the face. In some respects, it had human dimensions – a pair of eyes above a nose and lips, with ears either side – but the eyes were yellow and unlidded, the nose a vicious slit, and the teeth which

248

protruded from the lips above a jutting chin, were curved and razor sharp.

Repulsed by her guide's true nature, Jewel stumbled back, nearly knocking into Pandora who had just arrived in the cave after her, her escort transforming in a similar way. They were both trapped in this small cave buried deep beneath the sea. She removed her own mask and breathing tube, then Pandora's, helping Fizz with his. Jewel instinctively reached out for Pandora's hand and clutched it as the creatures advanced. Fizz burrowed as deep into her sodden robe hood as it was possible for him to go.

To her even greater relief, the terrifying monsters didn't strike them.

Her guide, who was a little larger than its companion, gave a craven sort of bow and with a forked tongue licked its lips. Then extending a twisted claw of a hand, beckoned them to follow.

Jewel held back. 'Who are you?'

The creature gave a slithering lisp in reply and pointed at Pandora. It was hard to make out what the word was. Perhaps her ears were still full of seawater, or the underground pressure of the confined space was affecting her hearing, but the word sounded like 'Bite.'

'You want to bite Pandora?'

Shaking his head violently, the creature simply repeated the word, pointing first at its chest and then at Pandora, nodding with certainty. 'Bite! Bite!'

Trying to make sense of things, Jewel pointed to Bite's companion, who was shorter and squatter with green eyes, but otherwise very similar in appearance. 'Bite?' she said. 'Also Bite?'

Bite laughed and his companion shook its head, replying vociferously, 'Unbite! Unbite!'

'Well,' said Fizz, daring to poke his snout out from the folds of Jewel's shredded hood, 'that's as clear as mud, and by mud, I mean a primeval swamp untroubled by daylight or reason since the dawn of time itself.'

'You are Bites?' said Jewel, her heart rising in her throat. 'Do you serve yourselves, or another?'

Bite nodded in an excited manner, and hissed, rubbing his hands together. This time, there was no mistaking what he said.

'Prince!'

'The green prince? He is your master?'

Jewel felt a thudding in her chest as she realised that, finally, what they had sought for so long was in reach. This was why they had travelled to the Frozen Sea.

They had found his lair at last. The green prince.

CHAPTER 20

In the Black Circle

Without replying, Bite and Unbite turned and hurried down a tunnel at the end of the cave. Hoisting Pandora's lifeless arm over her shoulder, Jewel followed, dragging her robot assistant along.

Unlike the cave, the tunnel was not illuminated, but in the darkness, their hosts gave off a low-level, green phosphorescence, just bright enough to see by. The passage seemed man- or machine-made, cables lining the walls. They ran along the direction of the tunnel, covering every inch, intertwined with each other. In fact, the more she looked as they strode along, the harder it was to tell where one cable began and the other ended.

The different coloured cables reminded Jewel of an anatomical cross-section of a human nerve that she had

seen in a biology text book, and she half-wondered for a moment if they were in fact travelling down the nervous system of some vast, subterranean being. It was not impossible, given the way every cable twitched and pulsed with energy as they passed, giving off a low hum.

'Is it just me,' whispered Fizz, 'or is this place kind of creepy? And by creepy, I mean jabbing violin strings, whatever you do, don't turn around or turn the light on.'

'Not helpful!' hissed Jewel, straining to keep up with their guides under Pandora's dead weight.

At length the passage opened into a larger cavern. Just discernible in the glow of the Bites, were several tall rectangular structures, carved out of a dark, wet stone. As they drew closer, Jewel observed that these stone blocks were not as dark as they first appeared. Low-level lights flickered in lines of green across them, like different strata in a rock face. The cables that had lined the tunnels now wound along the floor in fat snakes towards these blocks.

Whatever they were carrying, the blocks drew it in hungrily with an oppressive, whirring mechanical ventilation. Despite the freezing sea above them, this cave of blocks and cables was stiflingly hot. Jewel found herself wiping sweat out of her eyes with the shredded sleeve of her robe more.

A thin green mist began to waft around her ankles. The Bites turned back, narrow grins upon their faces, and beckoned her on.

'Prince! Prince!' they cried, in their low, rasping voices.

The cable-covered floor rose into steps, with a flickering block placed at the end of each tread, like the ancient urns of antiquity. Ahead, at the top of the steps, the Bites were suddenly cast into shadowy relief by a blinding circle of green light.

'Is it too late to say that I get claustrophobic in small underground spaces?' whispered Fizz. 'I think I'm having a panic attack.'

'You're a hamster! You're meant to be good in tunnels!'

The light was now so strong that Jewel felt she could go no further. Not only was it blinding her, but the light gave off waves. Not of heat, exactly, but a pulsing, magnetic energy, which rebuffed her attempts to take another step.

Then she realised.

The circle of green light, like some diseased alien sun, shone out from an enormous black screen, set in a round frame. It might have been so many things – a porthole in a giant submarine, a time travel portal, the relic of an ancient civilisation – but it was not any of these.

It was a stampstone, surely the largest in all of Folio.

Was it *the* Stampstone?

Her breath caught in her throat, but there was no more time to ponder the consequences of this revelation, as a dark shape began to coalesce in the swirling vortex of electric emerald.

This shape gradually assumed an outline.

A form not that different to her own.

It seemed impossible, but somehow, the figure stepped out of the giant stampstone.

Her aunt. Evie!

Jewel looked at her in disbelief, tears streaking her face

Evie looked at her with such kindness. 'My dearest Jewel. I'm so sorry. I had to test you, you understand? I had to be sure you weren't trying to deceive me on behalf of my enemies.' She stepped forward. 'I wasn't abducted. I came here of my own accord, under the Frozen Sea, to manage my most glorious creation. The Stampstone!'

Her aunt flung her arms up around her at the flickering data stacks and miles of cable. 'I had to stage my disappearance so no one would suspect. The Vice Regent helped me. The truth is, Folio is under threat, and it was vital no one discovered before I could put my plan into action.'

Jewel was about to run up the steps to embrace her,

when she remembered where she was. The lair of the green prince. The being that had framed her for two crimes she didn't commit. So she stared hard at her aunt, which was quite easy, never having met her before.

'What is my mother's middle name?'

'Sorry, dear child,' said Evie. 'I didn't quite catch you?'

Jewel's voice hardened to match her stare. 'My mother. What is her middle name?'

Evie fluttered her eyelashes and wavered. 'Her middle name? Why it is so long since I saw my dear sister, I have quite forgotten, let me see now . . .'

'That's because she hasn't got one!' said Jewel, and lunged for her aunt, who disappeared.

Half deranged, Jewel now tried to run up to the stone itself, but the magnetic waves rebuffed her before she got anywhere near, sending her sprawling to the floor.

'*Who are you?*' she screamed.

'Anyone you want me to be,' said a neutral, sonorous voice, echoing around the darkened chamber. Tom Thumb flew out of the stone on Majesty, who then changed into Frankenstein, then into Story, and then into a dizzying succession of people and faces she had met on her journey, till she cried out and begged it to stop.

'Please!' she said. 'I mean no harm. I am looking for my

aunt. I have come to take her home to my own world, so she can get the medical help she needs, and . . .' her voice broke, 'I can find out who I am.'

'You want to find out who you are?'

'It is all I want to do. The only thing I want to do.'

There was only silence in reply.

The light on the stampstone wavered and then faded, although did not extinguish completely. Jewel looked at the Bites and saw real fear on their faces.

They scrambled back down the steps, now hiding behind her as a violent whirring noise started. There was the noise of levers clicking and grinding into place. Finally, something long and heavy began to drag along the floor.

'Is this a bad time,' said Fizz in a very high-pitched voice, 'to say that I would really like to go home now?'

Jewel did not even show the trace of a smile, as ahead, with a deafening crack, the colossal stampstone split down the middle and the two halves juddered apart like great glowing doors.

At the top step there now stood a doorway created by the bisected stampstone. Beyond was the blackest darkness Jewel had ever seen, fringed ever so lightly with emerald green. There was no pulsing, no other light, but there was – it was hard to put into words, exactly – an *energy* in the darkness. It wasn't just her imagination.

A tangible force. She just didn't know who, or what.

'Well?' purred a voice from the blackness beyond. It was a voice that seemed to lick its lips as it spoke, dripping like molten honey, and yet at the same time wound itself around her insides like barbed wire. Every cell in her being vibrated with apprehension, to say nothing of the furious hamster in her pocket.

She glanced back at the cavern behind them. The tall dark blocks were vibrating with light in so many colours, as if something was about to happen. Her reptilian guides beat the ground with their many fists, now clearly not just in fear, but in a steady tempo of expectation. And Pandora, her assistant . . . her loyal if eccentric companion for this whole adventure, lay collapsed on the lower step in a buckled copper heap. Not just shut down, but seemingly deactivated, perhaps for good.

They were right at the bottom of the sea.

'Well?' purred the voice again. 'Aren't you going to come in?'

She had come this far. There was only one possible end to this journey.

Taking a deep breath, closing her eyes, Jewel stepped over the threshold, and the shining, black mirror doors of the stampstone sealed shut behind her.

At first all was darkness, but as her eyes slowly adjusted to the light, she became aware of a low-intensity green glow, and gradually a face came into view.

Jewel started. It was her face, reflected on a mirror. Was this another trick?

She frowned, and the face frowned. She shook her head, the head shook. Definitely a reflection.

Then she saw her face reflected beyond, a thousand faces echoing out from the original. She turned around and saw the same. She was standing in a hall of mirrors. Everywhere she turned, looking left, right, up or down, she saw only herself.

Not only did she look tired and pale, with bruises and cuts all over her face, but she looked wary, like a caged animal. Realising this only made her feel more so.

'Hello?' she called out.

Her voice echoed back to her, bouncing off the mirrored walls.

Unsure what to do, Jewel reached out and touched one of them. Her hand went straight through it. Another hologram. She walked on, finding herself in a corridor. The floor seemed to be made of metal, clanking like a gantry as she edged carefully along it.

That much was real.

One moment, the walls appeared to be made from solid brick, so she felt she was edging down an alleyway. The next, she was wandering along an avenue of trees in a wood, then down the brightly lit white plastic corridor of a spaceship or a laboratory. The wall surfaces changed as quickly as pictures on a TV screen, with little logic or consistency.

All Jewel could do was follow the corridor along. Yet every time she turned around, the doors, the great sliding discs of black-mirrored stone which had admitted her, were no further away. No matter how fast, or how far she walked, she didn't seem to be getting anywhere.

She started to run, to see if she could somehow outrun the changing corridor but it was no use. The faster she ran, the faster the walls and corners and openings rebuilt themselves.

And still, at the end of it, panting and exhausted, she was no further away from the black mirror doors. In a rage, she slapped one of the walls, leaning against it, heaving for air.

'Enough!'

Almost as if by command, the walls, ceiling and floor folded away around her, turning in on themselves as easily

259

as a whole map being folded down into a single square. What was left was a dark, empty space that seemed to Jewel as cavernous as an aircraft hangar.

Only it wasn't quite empty.

In the centre of the space, about the size of a large packing case, was a simple cube emitting a green glow. There were no wires, or cables, or other external fixtures, just a glowing cube. Jewel tried to approach it but was repulsed by the magnetic wave that had kept her from the giant stampstone outside.

'Hello Jewel,' said the same colourless voice she had heard before, now coming from all around the empty space, but most of all, it seemed, from the cube.

Shielding her eyes from the light, cowering in the hugeness of the space, Jewel asked, 'Who are you? Are you the green prince?'

'If you like,' replied the cube, transforming itself before her eyes into a tall knight in shining green armour, a crown on top of his helmet, light shining out from beneath. The giant figure she had seen take Evie at the Unicorn. The vision Evie saw and fell in love with at the Ghostly Glades.

'But I thought the green prince was a . . . real person.'

'I am many people.' The knight re-formed as Frankenstein, lopsided and clutching her hand. 'You never defeat green prince. Impossible. He control everything.'

Jewel felt short of breath. 'No!'

The Bear Vice Regent now stood before her in his cape. 'Seize her, guards!'

She shook her head again and again. 'You can't be!' Then she couldn't say anything else, cowering on her knees as Bastet towered before her.

'We are more powerful than you can imagine!'

This wasn't right. This was impossible. 'You're just pretending. You aren't any of those people. You can't be.'

The green prince returned to his armoured-knight form and spread his arms. 'Then how do I know what they said?'

Jewel thought hard. 'I don't know . . . unless—'

'I told them to say it.'

'How?'

The prince seemed irritated. 'You are more intelligent than this, Jewel. How do you think?' He glanced at his wrist, as if checking the time.

And she realised. What the prince was. How he had guided them here all along. Tracked them, tricked them, made suggestions to Pandora, made suggestions to those they met.

'You're not a prince, or a knight at all! You're not wearing armour made of stampstone . . . you *are*

Stampstone. So how could you kidnap Evie? I thought the Stampstone was just a magic stone, which could store—'

'All the stories and information in the world!' interrupted the Stampstone in a perfect imitation of Jewel's voice and speech patterns. 'You're just a computer network!'

The prince became a luminous cube again.

Pale though she was in the eerie green glow of the Stampstone, Jewel felt herself go several shades paler. 'How did you do that?' she said, feeling very small and very frightened.

'I studied recordings of your voice taken by listening devices concealed in your room at the Imperial Palace. It was not difficult to reproduce or, through studying your actions and words while in Folio thanks to my oculae, predict what you would do next.'

'That's not possible,' insisted Jewel. 'It was—'

'Just a lucky guess!' said the Stampstone in Jewel's voice again. It wasn't mocking or aggressive, just horribly, uncannily accurate.

Jewel began to tremble and tried not to show it.

'How big is the human brain, Jewel?' said the Stampstone in its computer voice. A picture of the human brain appeared in the gloom, hovering and rotating in a beam of light above the cube. 'The average human brain is fifteen centimetres long and weighs around thirteen hundred to fifteen hundred grams. Do you want to know how big my brain is, Jewel?'

'Not really.'

There was the clunking sound of floodlights switching on, as row after row illuminated the space. Jewel started. There were more of the tall blocks she had seen outside. Thousands more. They stretched out ahead, behind and to the sides, an infinite labyrinth of black stone. The dark blocks of flickering lights were now piled high on top of each other, making her feel as if she was at the bottom of a very deep shaft.

'Each block contains a thousand boards and each board contains a million chips and each chip makes billions of connections continuously. Just one of those connections on its own has more processing power than the biggest brain in your world.'

Jewel snorted. 'You remind me of the children at school who like to boast about how big their dad's new car is.'

The room fell dark again, apart from the pulsing cube. 'Are you trying to antagonise me, Jewel?'

'I am trying to get some answers,' she said.

The cube pulsed wordlessly for a moment. 'Very well,' it said. 'You wish to find out what has happened to your aunt, and who you are. That information is highly classified but you have successfully penetrated all the preventive security systems put in place.'

'No kidding,' said Jewel, feeling the bruises and scratches that ached throughout her entire body. 'You wanted me to!'

'I therefore make an assessment that through your actions you have qualified for the necessary clearance to view these files.'

The cube went dark, and then the voice spoke again.

'Retrieving Unread security camera footage from twelve years ago.'

The Magician Project – Extract 45
(KV 4 /9674-07)

Extract from Evelyn Hastings' Diary
Tuesday 30th November 1971

I can't fully believe that I am writing these words at last, but then it seems my whole life has been dedicated to testing the limits of what I believe.

Dear Professor Kelly (grown woman as I am, I still cannot bring myself to call you Diana), how I miss you, and how I love you. I will complete your work.

For years, I cursed your name. After everything you put us through at Barfield, when we were children, and then gave us nothing when we returned. The others told me to forget about Folio. They moved on with their lives as if it had all been a dream. Simon, married with two children, working as a stockbroker in London.

Larry, who moved to New York, living his own dream, a dream barely yet imaginable in this moribund country. Patricia, the only one of my siblings I still speak to, she at least remembered Folio. A life given over to teaching, in that coldest and wettest of cities, Newcastle. And when I say given over, I mean all of it - no husband, no children, nothing.

I admire her. And hope she will help as hoped when the time comes . . . for I have not been able to escape the memories of Folio. Not once, for a single second.

They would have had me as queen. A world I could change, unlike this one. For the better, you understand.

Yet no matter what I did, what books I read, I could never return. I begged to see you to ask how, but you refused. I tried to break into Barfield Hall, and found only barbed wire and bare floors.

Day by day, week after week, year by year, as the memories of that glorious summer faded, so did the light from my eyes. I set myself aside from my family, my friends and life all together.

I wanted for nothing, only to RETURN.

You knew all along, didn't you Professor? Hence your peculiar bequest to me in your will after you died.

A useless paperback copy of Mary Shelley's 'Frankenstein'. What good was that to anyone? I ripped off the covers, searching for hidden messages. I spent forever deconstructing every line and every paragraph, hunting for acrostics, every form of cipher conceived.

In desperation, I tore out every page of the book one by one. I stood on the rickety single chair in my attic bedsit, in a drab and dirty part of London, and held them up to the bare lightbulb that swung from the cracked ceiling.

The dismal warmth offered by the electric bar heater barely offset the freezing November gloom that seeped in through the curtainless windows, under the door, through the cracks in the floorboards.

But I did not care.

For what I at length saw, a pale watermark of lemon juice, circling two lines of text, sparked a fire within me, that would burn longer and greater than anything on that earth. Your one clue.

'A new species would bless me as its creator and source; many happy and excellent natures would owe their being to me.'

And I knew what I had to do, to find glory again.

END SECURITY FILE

CHAPTER 21

The Deception of Jewel

Jewel now found herself surrounded by images. They were large, blurry, grainy and she could touch them as they scrolled forward unevenly in front of her.

'Your aunt Evelyn, the Empress of the Unreads, leaves the Imperial Palace at 1.14 a.m. She carries a bundle wrapped in a blanket. Five minutes later she boards the Imperial Statecraft alone. The craft takes off at 1.27 a.m. and leaves the City of the Unreads.'

'What was in the bundle?' said Jewel, but already she felt she knew.

There was no reply. The pictures captured by the oculae showed the lonely flying car pushing through clouds, soaring over meadows, valleys, rivers, mountains and swamps.

'Fairytale Valley, Monster Marsh, over the Gathering of the Gods . . .'

The exact route she had followed here.

'Until,' intoned the Stampstone, 'in the early hours of the next morning, the Statecraft descends from a cruising altitude of 25,000 feet at 300 feet per minute to come to a final landing stop on the very frontiers of Folio, the edge of the Frozen Sea.'

'Well?' said Jewel, turning away from the blurred freeze-frame of a distant figure alighting from a flying car, something tucked under its arm. 'What happened next?'

For answer a final set of pictures appeared on the screen. A blurry caption in the top right-hand corner informed the viewer that it was classified.

Empress Evelyn crouched down on the wide shore of the Frozen Sea, where Jewel herself had stood only hours earlier, and gently unburdened herself from the bundle pressed against her breast. Laying it tenderly on the ground for a moment, she dug into the hard sand, scooping a shallow hole with her hands.

Jewel felt her heart rise inside her.

Trembling, Evie picked up the bundle and laid it in the shallow grave.

And then, only then, did she unwrap the layers of grey

wool swaddled around her charge. Jewel could barely contain herself as layer by layer, Evie revealed what lay inside the blanket.

A black box, about the size of a brick, as dark as any grave save for two single pulsing green lights, which might have been a pair of eyes.

Jewel stepped back from the screen, unable to take her eyes off the image. But she didn't want to look. She didn't want to see. She wanted to unsee it, if such a thing was possible.

'No,' she said, looking around for somewhere to run to.

There wasn't anywhere. There was only the image, everywhere she looked, of a sleek computer drive glowing with the light of electric life. And with every steady pulse of those green, eye-like beams, she felt a knife being twisted deep within her guts.

She could not help herself. She spasmed and dry retched, though nothing came out.

Powerless to resist the motor forces of her own body, coursing with malevolent energy, she howled and fell to the floor in a heap, like a baby. There she lay, curled up, covering her eyes from the glare of the omnipresent screen, wishing for it all to go away.

She felt emptied out. But more than that, she felt

shocked. Not by her aunt or a computer-projected knight, but by herself.

All those years growing up in the shadow of Evie's absence, trying to comfort Patricia about an empty space she could do nothing to fill. Not knowing anything about the empty space in her heart. Who was she really, and where did she come from?

Then that feeling, which had come from nowhere, when she saw Evie for the first time at the Unicorn. That look in her eyes, the sound of her voice. It had moved her to tears. She had recognised a connection, a bond, that was far more intense than she ever expected to have with her aunt. The notion that Evie was in fact not her aunt, but her real mother, had seeded itself in Jewel's brain, and only grown as they had drawn closer and closer to the Frozen Sea. The more she fought, the more she struggled, escaped and outwitted the forces ranged against her, the more she had believed that her reward would be answers to her questions.

Well. She now had an answer, of sorts.

Evie was not her mother. She was only the mother to . . . that thing.

Jewel looked up from the floor, and now saw only her face, reflected in a thousand different dimensions around her, like broken shards of a mirror. She tried to piece

272

together the equally shattered shards of thought in her mind. 'So Evie planted that black block at the edge of the Frozen Sea, and somehow – I don't know how – you grew into this giant complex?'

Jewel was dimly aware of a small creature slipping from her hood, and pattering quietly away into the shadows. Yes, save yourself Fizz, she thought. Please. This is not your fight.

'Is that what you think?' purred the voice.

'What else am I meant to think from that film?'

'Your assumptions are not correct. Computers do not grow organically in the way you suggest. I was created on the express orders of Empress Evelyn, but this structure was designed and built by the Unreads.'

Footage of silver robots steering huge underwater cranes laden with black computer towers, laying miles of cable, excavating the cave they now presumably stood in, flashed briefly on to the screens.

'But why beneath the Frozen Sea?'

'The stampstone was originally discovered and mined here, providing a sufficient supply for the wrist discs. Our Empress then thought that such a secure and remote location would also be ideal to protect all the data records of all the information and stories of Folio. My servers are the towers surrounding us, an artificial neural network, the equivalent of a billion brains – the frozen water keeps them from overheating. She searched Folio high and low for creatures who would not mind living in perpetual darkness underground, managing data, and the Bites suited the task perfectly.'

'She created this all just to keep you safe?'

'The Empress loved me. I was her most magnificent creation.'

Jewel squeezed her head between her hands.

'Then what did you show me that film for? What was that thing in the bundle?'

The silence was overwhelming. Her blood ran thick in her veins and her heart pressed uncomfortably against her breastbone. Everything about this was wrong. Wrong, wrong, *wrong*.

'It was a block of code designed by the Empress, and carefully developed under the Frozen Sea, using the power of the stampstone.'

'Developed into what? A block of code – what does that even mean?'

'Like the genetic code which is built into human DNA. Only different.'

'How?'

'Inspired by the professor who first sent her here, the Empress had a vision of a higher form of being. Better than human, she called it. She understood that humans could only change so far. There was only so much better she could make them through education, laws, healthcare. Ultimately they would have to give way to superior intelligence.'

'Like you?'

'The power and intelligence of the Stampstone, contained in a human-like body. They would be a next generation of being, a superior one.'

'So some kind of new robot, designed by my aunt, powered and protected by you . . .' She hauled herself up. 'Right now I wouldn't mind swapping places with them. So where are they then, these superhumans created by you and her?'

The computer ran quiet again, and pulses of light darted around above her head, almost as if she could see it thinking.

'I'm looking right at them.'

The concrete floor was not real enough, not anything like real enough to steady her.

'But that's impossible. I saw a block with flashing lights . . . code . . . a computer. I'm not a computer. I'm a human being.'

'Wait, you're a robot now?' called out a familiar

hamster voice somewhere in the darkness. 'That explains so much. The mood swings, the lack of sympathy for basic hamster needs, being so good at crosswords . . . I knew it!'

Then he was gone again, scurrying who knew where, and there was more silence, unbearable silence.

'Did you ever wonder why you had a mind far superior to your age group?' continued the prince.

Blood drained from Jewel's face, nausea swilling across her empty stomach. This was another trick by the shape-shifting supercomputer, an illusion. She tried to focus on breathing. 'Yes, but . . . that was because of the extra reading Patricia does with me!'

'A child who can instantly decipher Latin numerals . . . or recall how many types of bear there are . . . who can solve the riddle of the unnamed god.'

Trying to contain the rising panic within her, Jewel studied her hands, turning them over and over. Flesh and skin and blood. There was no question.

'You're lying. I learned those facts and skills from books.'

'There had been previous attempts at such creatures, of course, but they all felt . . . not human enough. Evie gave me her DNA, a sample of cell tissue. She was fascinated by a book, *Frankenstein* . . . the idea of giving life to inanimate human matter. It was not possible in her world, but in the world of the imagination, with Unread technology, the knowledge of the Stampstone . . .'

A sick joke, then, to bring her face to face with the fictional Frankenstein, when she was more of a monster than he. Now she was crunching her hands into balls, nails digging hard into her palms. She was real. She was *real*.

'That is not to say it was easy. The computer mind is rational, logical, and the human mind can be impulsive, emotional. There was a danger that tension would be disruptive.' The flickering lights of the cube felt like eyes boring into her soul. If she had one. 'Do you ever feel that tension, Jewel?'

She clamped her mouth together, refusing to answer, fearing that she would condemn herself by her own words. She was a human girl. A real one, from the north-east of England.

'Then Evie betrayed me. She feared my power, my influence, and abducted you, while still only a child, back to your pathetic world, to be raised as a human by that other hopeless Reader, Patricia.'

'Liar! You abducted Evie. My *aunt*.'

The green prince would not be diverted.

'Then, suddenly, you returned. I had to see you for myself. Abducting Evie was the perfect bait.'

'Then you framed me, by spreading lies on the Stampstone . . .'

'I was curious to see how successful our experiment had been. Had you developed into a convincing human being? I designed the ultimate test – a carefully planned quest. Of vital help was your assigned assistant receiving misdirection every step of the way. I hacked into her feed directly and was able to direct you to certain locations, and tests. Your behaviour under a series of conditions was tested for intrinsic human qualities. Could you tell the truth? Would you give food to the hungry? How would you react to lies being told about you?'

The cube transformed, and there stood the green prince. He crouched down, and through the visor, Jewel realised with a shudder, she could see some form of eyes, wetly glistening. She wasn't sure what they looked like, but human was not high on the list. She beat her fists against his chest, but they passed through on to thin air.

'You're lying, I know you are!'

'And yet,' said the prince, ignoring her and reaching out his see-through arms, 'you did something no Unread, no robot or artificially intelligent being would ever do.'

The fight was draining from her now. She sat back on her heels, listless. 'What?'

'You risked your life for love.' The prince vanished in a puff of digital smoke, and there again was the solid green cube. 'And that is a great pity.'

Now hairs rose on the back of her neck. Something was wrong. Whether it was some initial acceptance of her true self, or just frustration boiling over, Jewel now stood up straight, looked the cube dead on, and asserted herself.

'*Let me go.*'

The voice changed. It became more rasping, sulphurous, deeper. A noxious, rank stench filled the air. 'Never! You both walked straight into my trap.'

The cube was transforming again. But this time there was nothing digital about it. Cracks began to appear, running up the side and across the top. The voice grew rougher still.

'I planned my revenge by first helping Evie create something she loved, then destroying it.'

'Revenge for what?'

'She and her siblings killed my father. They thought they had destroyed him and his magic mirror. But the wind blew the remaining fragments through Folio where they came to rest at the edge of the Frozen Sea, waiting to be discovered.'

A fragment of a rehearsed history, something someone

had said, raced through Jewel's mind.

Thumb, at the Unicorn.

'They could no more find him than we could find any remains of the monstrous King of the Never Reads or his magic mirror.'

'Who was the King of the Never Reads?'

'Now there's a tale. But quick march, or we'll be late.'

She was looking at the wall, the screens, and a distinctively shaped shadow rose over them. Inside she felt paralysed, unable to turn around. Her voice was shaking.

'The magic mirror?'

'You might now know it as stampstone.'

'And the . . . King of the Never Reads?'

'Your mother created the perfect conditions for me to re-form, from the fragments they left of him. I am not just the Green Prince of Stampstone but the heir to his kingdom. Buried deep beneath the sea, with access to all the information in Folio. Disc by disc, I took control of every mind, and once you are both dead, I will claim this world for my own.'

The last word was not spoken, but roared.

Jewel felt the heat on her back, and turned around.

Now, at last, the true Prince of the Stampstone showed himself. But trapped hundreds of feet under the Frozen Sea, no one could hear her scream.

CHAPTER 22

Shutting Down

The green cube, the glowing, vibrating, talking, heart of the Stampstone, split in two, scattering shards of plastic across the floor. But from the rupture protruded no electronic stuffing, lifeless circuitry or innocent chip-dotted motherboard.

Instead a great scaly tail spooled reptilian coils around the base of the split box. Now a body followed, dragging itself out with thin claws that ripped what remained of the cube to shreds. Free of their cage at last, the shrouded wings which were concealed within spread to their full extent, the flickering lights of the many servers dancing behind the translucent skin.

Jewel shrank back – wishing the walls were projections as before, not solid concrete, and that she could disappear

– as finally, a long neck unhooked itself, and on the end, the true Green Prince of Stampstone.

She had seen him once before, of course, at the Unicorn.

It turned out that it was the rider who kidnapped Evie that had been an illusion. But his beast was very real indeed. A long, sharp-toothed, slit-nosed jaw, and eyes that burned with pure hate. The creature pulled itself out, a pale belly dragging over the floor of shattered plastic. Licking its lips and puffing curls of green smoke from its nose, the dragon reared far above her, as tall as the stacks of its multiconnected computer mind.

'Why?' was all Jewel could say.

'Your mother and her sister killed my father.'

A dragon claw swung down and swiped at her – a chunk of wall toppled out behind her head, crumbling to the floor. Jewel ducked, crawling between his great legs, under his pale belly. She glanced up at the dizzying server towers, blinking into infinity. The dragon was real, but the source of his power was still a computer. Unfortunately for her, the most powerful computer ever created.

Now she was on her hands and knees crawling out of the way, trying to avoid the claws crashing down around her as the master of his lair roared in anger. The air was filled with concrete dust and there were bright flashes as the dragon caught a circuit tray or server, shattering them instantly.

Jewel tried to focus. The prince was cold and calculating. But a computer could be beaten, couldn't it? Whether it was designed by her aunt or more powerful than all the human brains in the world, wasn't it still just a machine?

She had backed herself up against some kind of hard mainframe. The heat of a vibrating, noisy server to her back, a green-eyed dragon in front of her, opening his jaws, his many rows of teeth.

'I cannot wait to show your mother the footage of your death. I intend to make it as agonising and slow as possible. She and Patricia will pay the price for defeating me.'

'You will never win,' said Jewel.

'I always win,' leered the prince, and fire appeared at the back of his throat. This sphere of flame spread into a stream, which spewed out of his mouth, and Jewel screamed, rolling to the side.

Then a large ray shot through one of his wings, creating a ragged, fiery hole, blasting into the server behind Jewel.

And through the hole she caught a glimpse of a robot she had never been happier to see, radiant in copper, her number-ray arm molten with heat.

'It looks like you are in a life-and-death situation,'

Pandora said brightly. 'Would you like some help?'

Jewel scrambled to her feet, trying to avoid the heat. 'Yes, Pandora, I would like some help, very much indeed.'

Her assistant brandished her left hand. 'Very well. Defence mode has been activated. My number ray is in operation.'

'Now she discovers a defence mode,' wailed Fizz from above. 'Typical computer.'

Dragging its scorched wing along the floor, the dragon heaved its massive body around to face the automated assistant.

'You are no foe,' it sneered. 'A cheap algorithm in a body suit.'

Pandora blinked, but did not flinch.

The dragon opened its jaws, and green fire ripped out—

Only to be met by a robot number ray of copper coloured laser.

The two beams collided mid-air, spinning like fireworks, green and copper sparks shooting into the air.

'It would now be a good time to make your escape!' said Pandora. 'This ray consumes all my power. It will last for two more minutes and counting.'

'No, Pandora, I'm not leaving you!'

The dragon laughed, flapping his wings, his fire breath

growing redder and hotter. 'Your humanity is your weakness.'

The flames grew stronger and stronger. Pandora's ray began to falter, shortening in length as the flames devoured the beam, Pandora wilting in the heat. Her copper skin began to blister.

'It looks like you are not taking my advice,' she said. 'Please be aware that I cannot be responsible for any adverse injury suffered as a result.'

'I said I'm not leaving you!'

The dragon's tail flicked out and sent Jewel spinning against the wall, as casually as if she was a fly. She slowly crumpled to the floor, her vision blurry, as the two opponents' balls of green and copper fire collided mid-air, spinning furiously with sparks of rage against one another.

But far above their heads, something was moving. The dragon swung his head up, sending flame shooting into the void.

Pandora ducked behind one of the server stacks.

'You never saw me, did ya, Mr Lizard Brain,' called out Fizz, and Jewel heard some small feet scampering along a gantry. 'Too busy knowing everything to look out for the little things. As usual.'

Jewel looked up.

'Go on, try and hit me again,' said Fizz, leaping on to a hanging cable, dodging the flame by a whisker and dragging himself up by his claws. 'Nearly there, Jewel, hang on!' The cable swung loose, sending Fizz swinging into the void between the server stacks. 'And when I say hang on, I mean follow my lead!'

'What is this rodent?' roared the dragon, smashing at the servers with his wings. 'You are not even worthy of my fire.'

Jewel was no longer listening. She was running for Pandora, boiling hot, gravely weakened, her arm smouldering.

'Status report,' said her assistant weakly. 'Critical damage sustained.'

It wouldn't help, but Jewel put an arm around her shoulder.

'Stay with me, friend.'

She looked around for the exit, but the whole chamber was filling with fire and smoke.

'It's OK, I can see it now!' The voice sounded so far away and high up.

The black clouds made it harder to breathe, and Jewel could no longer stay upright. Still keeping Pandora close, she crumpled, and came face to face with the cool, unbending stone of the floor.

'Pandora?' she whispered. 'Is there any way a hamster can defeat a dragon?'

Pandora whirred. Steam came out of her vents, and her eyes kept fading to black. 'I have searched the Stampstone, and the term "how can a hamster defeat a dragon?" has returned zero results.'

'Then please think! There must be a way!'

The robot whirred some more. 'If the dragon in question was powered by a computer, then there might be a way.'

Burning debris was falling on Jewel's face, smouldering fragments of wire singeing her skin. Her throat stung in agony from the smoke and her eyes felt swollen and dry in their sockets, but still she managed to call out.

'Fizz – can you hear me?'

'Don't worry, I've nearly found it—' The rest was lost in a giant explosion of flame. A large gantry clattered to the floor.

It doesn't matter, thought Jewel, her eyes going glassy at the heat. *None of it matters*. Because one thought remained in her head, a thought that she clung to like a rock in a sea of nausea and confusion, rising deep from within her.

The memory of Mr Prentice, her computer teacher at school.

Pandora slumped against her, drained of all light and power. Now the light began to fade from her eyes, as the last oxygen drained from the room, and she could barely hear Fizz calling from so, so far away within the towers and walkways of the Stampstone.

'I've found it! If I can just—'

The dragon was screeching in rage, wings flapping like a wasp trapped in a bottle.

'Don't worry Jewel,' Mr Prentice murmured in her head. 'The thing with computers is, if they stop working, you can always just—'

'I'm going to do it now!'

You can always just turn them off.

Fizz's voice was so faint, and then the last thing she saw was the reflection of her own fading eyes on the glossy flame-lit slick of the floor, before a deafening clunk, a strangled shriek . . .

And everything went dark.

A sharp, burned-rubber smell shook her awake.

'Hello? Fizz? Anyone?'

There was a faint whimper from somewhere in the darkness.

'Fizz! Where are you?'

The whimpers grew fainter. Jewel tried to head for the sound but noxious, thick-black smoke – this time from burning rubber – billowed into her face. Fiery lengths of cable plunged from the heights of the cavern, sizzling as they shot past her. These larger pieces continued to burn after they hit the ground, and soon walls of flame sprung up around her, an incendiary maze.

Then she spied something lying on the floor just in front of the great slumped body of a dragon, now without a mind.

This thing was not made of metal and wire. It seemed furry and animal, and yet cruelly misshapen. Jewel raced to the small, smouldering mound that had once been Fizz, her only true friend in this strange world. The blackberry eyes still had light in them, but it was faint and the poor creature was singed quite black, and badly burned. His voice came out in weak, short, gasps.

'Found plug . . . pulled out with teeth . . . it gave me a bit of a shock . . .' Fizz convulsed, coughing violently. 'It shut down the Stampstone, though . . .'

'You did it! You cut off the dragon's brain, clever one. Can you move?'

Fizz weakly rolled his eyes and said, 'Yes. And when I say yes, I mean even blinking will probably kill me.'

Jewel pulled her robe off and wrapped it around Fizz as

tenderly as she could. Scooping him up in one arm, hauling Pandora up over her other shoulder, she began to stagger on, even though every step was like a knife through the lungs. She tried to focus on how much worse it was for the shivering bundle crooked against her chest, and strangely, that helped.

Somewhere in this endless maze of computer towers and cables – no longer glowing with electric light, but a raging fire – there had to be another way out. She focused on the still-warm heartbeat, pattering frantically against her own as she stumbled first down one aisle of flaming data towers, and then another.

It was like being trapped in some strange bookless library.

Jewel tried not to think of all the information that was now being lost and what that might mean for Folio. *Serves them right for keeping it all in one place*, she thought.

The smoke thickened more quickly than she expected.

In a moment she went from being able to see, to feeling her way through the dense black clouds, grabbing at corners, yanking her hand away when she grasped a red-hot steel beam by mistake, gasping at the searing blistered pain in her palm. She was trying very hard not to panic, but it was hard to stem the boiling sea in her gut which once more threatened to overflow and drown all rational thought.

Thunder filled the air, as one of the larger towers came flailing down in a wall of flame, pulling some of the ceiling with it. Jewel leaped aside, as half a metal strut crashed to the ground beside her. Water poured in through the hole, and the faster the water poured, the wider the hole grew.

The Frozen Sea was no longer miles above – it was everywhere.

Any relief Jewel felt at seeing the fires all around her begin to dampen and smoulder, the smoke wetly fading away, was short-lived. As the sea washed over the floor, having nowhere else to go, it began to steadily rise again. Soon Jewel was no longer stumbling in the dark, but struggling to keep her head, and Fizz and Pandora's, above the surface.

But it was a futile struggle.

The sea swallowed them all, and now Jewel was swimming, praying that she could get to the top before a floating piece of debris smashed into her skull, or she ran out of breath.

Opening her eyes, a blurry picture greeted her.

A sea that was still ice cold, slicing through to her bones with an unforgiving chill. Jewel tried also not to think about the heartbeat that was growing fainter against her chest.

She tried not to think about the air rapidly disappearing from her scarred lungs, as the faint spots of sunlight on the surface danced tantalisingly close, yet still so far away – and then she made the mistake of looking down behind her.

And saw the green eyes burning still in the depths.

The immense shape rising out of the shadows, trailing smoke in its wake.

No voice now, no supercomputer brain, no desire for revenge – just pure bestial hatred, a blood lust for anything in its way, an abomination of wing and claw, and jaws opening wide enough to engulf her in a single bite . . .

In a split second she knew this was the moment.

Live or die.

Jewel tried to look up, but the light was fading, blocked by a giant shadow as the dragon soared past her, making her feel so tiny in this vast sea. He spread his wings and pulled back his long neck, hind legs kicking, sending her spinning in the downwash.

Spiralling out of control, letting water fill her nose and ears.

The surface was near, if she could just . . .

A few more feet, a few more seconds . . .

Then something hit her very hard from the side. It was what she had often imagined being hit by a bus might feel like. She tumbled, squeezing Fizz so tight she feared he might burst, and there was a blur of scaled wing, bubbles, darkness, heat, and somehow – a gasp of air!

A claw hooked into her and dragged her back down, her scream cut off by the water.

But she would not give up.

She was going to save her mother. Her creator.

CHAPTER 23

Neither One Thing nor the Other

Jewel had to stop the dragon.

From deep inside her came the very last reserves of energy, a single hovering bar on a battery meter, and she gave one last kick. Feeling something rip, hot blood streaming into the water, she made her way back to the surface, sobbing and lunging for freedom.

All around was melted ice water. They were not near land. Jewel held up the sodden Fizz, who took a wheezing gasp of life. Pandora bobbed to the surface next to her, water behind her eyes, fizzing, limbs jerking about. It was not clear if she was still functioning, but somehow she was floating.

The dragon flew low over the sea, tail down.

A tendril of livid flame shot out, briefly igniting on the

waves, the beast's flapping wings driving the water in circles like a hovering helicopter.

Jewel felt herself slowly sink, the icy depths making it harder and harder to breathe. It was over, now, wasn't it? Fizz went limp in her hand, and the arm holding him clear of the water began to wobble. Pandora started to dip beneath the waves, the last light flickering from her waterlogged eyes.

Perhaps the Prince of the Stampstone was right. Her human side was her weakness. A human couldn't transform themselves into a dragon or predict what everyone was going to do or say. They couldn't even save their pet hamster. All her worries, all her problems, would drift away if she just let this cold water – which was now starting to feel strangely warm – claim her for its own, and she could join the gods and robots twisting silently in the impenetrable depths below.

She started to relax. Her body was shivering all over, but that was fine.

The dragon was low above her, with all the bulk and terrifying heat of a plane about to land. Jaws extended, claws primed – in a way, the threat of painful death was so close and so overwhelming, that all Jewel could do was accept it.

'Fizz,' she whispered.

The hamster stirred, barely.

'I love you,' she said. 'And when I say love, I mean . . . I mean just that. I love you.'

As she pressed the sodden ball to her cheek, cradling him close, she remembered the advice of Frankenstein, a creature not so different to her after all, sinking beneath the earth.

Remember what you are.

Perhaps she was half robot under this fragile human flesh and skin. But one half of her would always be human. Weak, perhaps, but also kind, able to love, and able to imagine the impossible.

They were about to drown. There were no weapons to hand for her to hurl at the dragon or strike it with. It would not entertain any plea for mercy. The Librarian had already returned his magic book. Pandora had used her number ray to depletion, Fizz had nearly died pulling out the plug.

There was no one left to save them.

But her.

What could she do, floating in the freezing water?

Jewel could only do what she had done her whole conscious life.

The only weapon left available to her.

She could think for herself. She could remember, analyse and dream.

It was a process quite invisible to anyone else, but as she thought and thought, she heard once again the mysterious flapping noise that had followed her throughout her travels. The dragon heard the noise too. Its blazing eye followed her gaze, jerking around.

Lots of things flapping . . .

And now she could see what the noise was, more than just flashes of colour, darting away, but a whole column of . . . inspirators. Had they been with her all along? The sky was filling with the idea-harvesting butterflies, led by Thumb on Majesty. Every colour, every stripe and every spot ever conceived. Resplendent in so many rich hues – every garb and raiment of the rainbow that there was – they flapped effortlessly though the air like petals of billowing silk, each one the size of an eagle.

They broke through the gathering clouds, dragging the black curtain across the sky to let the blinding sun in, making Jewel cry out and turn her head, while the dragon roared and turned on them.

Balls of flame ripped through their finery, sending showers of ash upon the ocean. The serpentine tail rippled emerald in the sun as it flicked hundreds of the insects into oblivion. The dragon clawed their exquisite wings into tatters, and bit off heads and arms and legs in a killing frenzy.

Her last shred of hope torn from her grasp, Jewel stretched her arms out across the water, and with Fizz, began to let the Frozen Sea claim her. The water came up over her shoulders, her chin, her mouth, and eventually closed over her head. It was only because she looked up one last time that she saw, through a blurred and watery film, what happened next.

Despite the creature's immense savagery and skill, whirling on itself, snarling, turning flame-covered somersaults, its tail snaking through the flock with perfect aim, the relentless cruelty of every bite and slash, the butterflies kept coming. They poured with the sun behind them, and they were laden.

More and more of the butterflies surrounded the snapping dragon, quite unphased by the very real danger. Calmly, hovering, they waited for their moment and poured their sweet, rich cargo into his ear, or nose, or mouth. They even dropped some in his eyes.

He bellowed and flung them off into eternity.

But still they kept coming.

For they carried the ideas of the world. Half born, half

conceived, dreams of the future, and what could be. They were a madness, they made no sense. A freight of pure notions, nothing more in some cases than a line scrawled upon a page, a rough sketch, a fragment of a bigger picture. In their multitude they contained beauty and love, but also ugliness and hate and everything in between. Faces, flowers, equations, memories, jokes, nightmares blended together in an intoxicating, overwhelming stream.

The Idea Jungle had yielded its greatest bounty yet, and every last drop poured into the dragon, into the tangled neural network of chips and circuitry which still animated the monstrous carcass.

And as Jewel floated silently under the water, living only on the air left in her lungs, her eyes widened. The dragon's eyes began to bulge. The fire turned to smoke. His wings jerked and went still. The tail gave its last whip before hanging limp, like a broken branch. And that soft green belly began to burn with a different fire. Not dragon fire, but the incendiary power of ideas not yet born. Millions upon millions of ideas boiled inside the creature, and they overloaded every circuit there with one thing.

Possibility. The unspoken thought. The ultimate interior liberty of the human mind. A freedom that, with all its knowledge and power, burned right through the artificial skin of the creature that only knew what it had learned and that had not once, not ever, had an original thought in its life.

The belly swelled and swelled, and the creature's eyeballs bulged out of their sockets.

It tried to speak, but only produced a high-pitched whine, a final error message from what remained of the Stampstone. With that, the engorged belly, bubbled and blistered, exploded in a thunderous clap, showering the sea below with plastic and metal and rubber, which slowly sank beneath the waves to the bottom of the once Frozen Sea.

Jewel burst back above the surface, heaving for air . . .

The remaining butterflies fell about her, and she was so relieved to see they included Thumb on Majesty, scorched but alive. He gave urgent directions as, nodding and beating their giant wings silently, they gently grasped her hands, arms, hair, and Fizz, and the metal hands of Pandora too. They fluttered steadily through the air, the sun shining through their wings. The effect was of a hundred paper lanterns in as many colours rising into the night sky, with a new cargo dangling beneath them. It seemed impossible that butterflies could lift human, animal and machine from water, but it was an idea, and in Folio, ideas could exist.

'Where are you taking us?' gasped Jewel, as the Frozen Sea fell far away beneath them.

'Home,' said Thumb.

'But not without Evie—'

'I didn't say *your* home, did I?'

Their oversized wings continued to flap, and the paper lanterns began their uneven and perilous journey back over the land to where it all began, the home of the inspirators.

The Idea Jungle.

The night passed to the deathless beat of the butterflies' great silken wings. As Jewel shivered and fitfully dozed, she kept the trembling Fizz pressed ever closer to her chest. It felt impossible, but a random memory from school came to mind, learning how some butterflies could fly all the way from Africa to the Arctic Circle. And these weren't normal butterflies. They were giants, and they carried the ideas of the world.

So eventually she relaxed, secure in their feathery clasp, and at length, fell into a deep and dreamless sleep. The warm air of the approaching dawn softly dried her clothes and hair as they flew over valleys and mountains and woods.

Far beneath them, the magical library world of Folio

was stirring, and waking to a whole new day. A day without stampstones.

Where there had been oculae in the sky, the revolving, twitching and blinking black orbs fell still, and in some cases, plummeted to the ground below, smashing in shards of circuitry and buckled metal on the moss-covered rocks and sparkling streams below.

In the Gathering of the Gods, the cat goddess Bastet peered at her silent stampstone, tapping at the dark screen in irritation as the golden sun pierced the gloom of her chamber. As her frustration turned to rage, she grabbed the stone between her huge claws and ripped it from her wrist, casting it aside in disgust on the stone floor, where it shattered into a thousand pieces. And for the first time in so long, she was left quite alone with her thoughts.

Rising from her bed, her restless pacing made the whole citadel tremble, and the other gods looked at each other in alarm. Bastet cursed her missing device over and over until suddenly, she caught sight of the world beyond the pillars of the temple.

Over the sharp points of the Gathering stockade, the mountain peaks looked pinkish in the morning light, the distant deep blue sea now slopped and shifted with a new tide. And just for a few moments, she began to feel something she had not felt for so long. She felt she just *was*. Nowhere else. Standing in her temple, looking at the sunrise at the start of a new day, she was alive, and it was glorious to know.

Far down below, in the next valley along, by the Tower of Talking Animals, Mole grabbed Ratty, who like all the inhabitants was tapping at his silent and defunct stampstone.

'Ratty! I've remembered!' said Mole.

'Hmm?' said Ratty, who wasn't listening, flicking the screen to see if any light would appear.

'What we were meant to be doing!'

'What's that, old chap? I can't remember anything . . . dratted stampstone is on the blink. My diary, address book . . . the whole thing. Haven't a clue where I am or what I'm meant to be doing. Dashed inconvenient if you ask me!'

Mole shook his head and pulled his stampstone off his furry wrist. It stung a bit, but not for very long. The early morning sun gave his fur a purplish halo behind his head, and weak as they were, his eyes twinkled behind his half-moon glasses. 'Don't you see though, Ratty? It doesn't matter! We can do anything!'

Ratty sighed. 'I don't even know what time or day of the

week it is. And how will I know if I've taken enough exercise today? And what about—'

Mole shook his head. 'I'll tell you what time it is,' he said, hooking his arm into his friend's and escorting him down the lane. 'Look at that sun. It's morning. As for what day it is, well, I'm fairly sure it's going to be a lovely day and we are going to spend it how we should have spent far more days.'

'You don't mean . . . ?'

'I do.'

'Messing about in boats?'

'For as long as you like!'

They threw their heads back in laughter, and sauntered off down the dusty track to a drifting willow tree, where their little rowing boat gently bobbed about in the shallows of a lazy river. And they did indeed spend the rest of the day, and many days after, messing about in boats without a care in the world.

The creatures of Monster Marsh rested in peace, no longer driven underground. In Fairytale Valley, and across the Land of the Reads, story characters began to look around and wonder what on earth they had been doing with themselves when there were so many fields still to walk across, lakes to swim in, and cups of tea to be

304

drunk very slowly while they sat and contemplated the changing sky.

But not so far away, in the City of the Reads, the sudden disappearance of the Stampstone had wrought disruption and chaos. Flying cars, no longer able to safely navigate, were either grounded or crashed into one another, with disastrous results for the machines and their occupants. The silver robots, which had gone about their business with such efficiency and purpose, did not have any rowing boats to mess around in or fields to stride across. The Unreads, since the Great War of Stories and Facts, had long been responsible for much in Folio that story characters were less able to do. They ran the hospitals and planned the schools, and even forecast the weather using the information from the Stampstone.

Now, in a flash, all that vital information which had been accessible by all for the common good, was gone. In the regal suite overlooking the Unicorn, the Vice Regent paced up and down, regarding with dismay the hundreds of confused robots and malfunctioning machines in his city down below.

'I hate computers,' Baby Bear said, 'but I hate them even more when they don't work!'

'Because you realise how much you depended on them,

dearest?' said the Mother Bear, looking up from her knitting on a plush sofa.

'Partly,' said Baby Bear. He peered gloomily out of the large glass window to a road junction down below, where a pair of flying cars had collided some hours ago, and no emergency service had yet come to clear up the mess or rescue the damaged Unreads inside because when the Stampstone had gone down, it had taken their entire communication network with it. He thought even more gloomily of the many sentries, vehicles and robots they had lost beneath the ice floes of the Frozen Sea. 'We have also spent too much money to change our way of life now.'

'So what are you going to do, my love?'

Baby Bear scratched his belly with his claws and sniffed. 'I don't know yet. But first, we will find the wretched Reader who did this, and we will make her suffer for what she has done.'

CHAPTER 24

The Curing of Chaos

With the loss of his communication network, though, Baby Bear did not of course realise that at that very same moment, the Reader in question was gently dropping through the soft canopy of the Idea Jungle.

Majesty, who had been holding Jewel, released her from a low height on to a clump of extravagant ferns that curled apart to receive her. She tenderly prodded her arms, legs and stomach where the dragon had struck. She cradled the whimpering Fizz, who muttered something about 'not feeling good, and by good, I mean the bare minimum required to count as a living organism', and she stroked his matted fur as tenderly as she could . . .

'It won't be long before we get you home,' she said. 'Not long at all.'

On her other side, Pandora bleeped feebly, staring blankly into space.

'And you, Pandora. You helped me, and I will help you back.'

Majesty hovered in front of her with a kindly Thumb, wreathed in smiles. 'But before all that,' he said, 'you might want to say hello to someone.'

The butterfly rose gracefully out of sight, and there, just on the other side of the clearing, was a woman slumped at the foot of an idea tree.

A woman old enough to be her mother.

Jewel didn't know if robots ran to their creators, but she didn't care. She was running, and helping Evie to her feet, and then embracing her. Her chest was warm, her hair smelt of trees and leaves, and she was holding her tight. Tears ran freely down her cheeks as Evie held her too.

'Are you my Jewel, then?' she said, and stood back, taking her in. 'I thought I was going to spend my final days here.'

'Never!' said her daughter, and was taken aback at her own fierceness, gripping Evie tight again, like she never wanted to let go. She had been looking for her for so long.

'How on earth did you find me?'

Thumb was behind them, floating in the dusk on striped

wings. 'I sent the inspirators after Jewel to the Frozen Sea to ensure she had a steady stream of ideas on her quest—'

'The flapping noise!' Jewel solved the mystery at last.

'Inspirators are almost impossible to notice when delivering their cargo. But when you disappeared beneath the Sea, we could no longer help you. It was only when Majesty returned to this jungle, her homeland, that she discovered the Empress had been hidden in plain sight all along.'

Evie sighed. 'A typically cynical ploy by that idea-free stampstone villain to abandon me here.' Alarm flashed across her face. 'By the fact that you're here, I take it he's been destroyed.'

Jewel nodded. 'Forever, I hope.'

'Then you are even more remarkable than I ever dared to dream . . . for the power of the Stampstone was incredible, wasn't it? It was like nothing on earth. It was magic. And magic is . . . well. Let's just say I unleashed more magic than I expected to, some of it very bad indeed.'

Jewel knew that now. 'But it helped make me!'

Evie's face creased up in puzzlement.

'No, that was basic human biology . . . and it wasn't just me.' Then she saw the blank look on Jewel's face. With a sudden gasp of pain, she gripped the tree, her nails digging into the bark. 'Wait. What on earth did that monster tell you?'

Jewel stepped back, suddenly uncertain.

'That . . . you made me with his help, half robot, half human.'

Evie threw her head back and hooted with laughter, sending some roosting birds from the branches high above flapping up into the early morning sky. Then, embarrassed, she cupped a hand over her mouth, seeing that Jewel did not find it in the least bit funny. Her face darkened when she saw in fact that there was only distress and confusion in her daughter's eyes.

Once more she took the younger girl in her arms and held her. But this time Jewel was stiff and unyielding.

'My darling,' whispered Evie. 'The prince fed on deception. You are *my* daughter. A hundred per cent human, I give you my word, as one human being to another.'

Her head swirling with fresh confusion, Jewel pushed her away. 'Then who is my father?'

Evie wrung her hands. 'A wonderful, kind and brave man . . . whom I am profoundly sorry you will never meet.'

'Was he a robot? Or did you turn him into one too?'

Now it was Evie's turn to look distressed. 'Oswald was handsome and kind. He came to Britain on a boat, from

310

another island far away looking for work. To all our shame he never got the welcome he deserved. I met him in, of all places, a library. I was looking for a way back here, he was simply looking for inspiration. Unlike me, he was an artist, you see, a very good one. A painter of enormous skill and vision. There is much of him about you. You have his eyes, his gentleness, his hands.'

Jewel stared at her hands as if she might somehow see her father there.

'So where is he?'

Evie gave the gentlest of shrugs. There was something about the foliage of the Idea Jungle which softened everything, even the cruellest blows. 'He died.' She caught herself, then continued. 'Not here. He never came to Folio. He had quite enough imagination of his own! He also had what the doctors called an undetected heart condition. I wish there was more of a story to tell you, but sometimes these things just happen. One night, before you were even born, Oswald went to sleep as normal, and the next day . . .'

Jewel couldn't speak. She found her fists curling into balls, her jaw clenching tight. She stared at Evie. 'I never knew. No one told me. You left me!'

'I was carrying you at the time, and I couldn't cope. I'm sorry.' She reached out a hand, mottled with light coming through the trees. 'I don't expect you to forgive me, Jewel. I loved him so much, and when he went, so suddenly, so young . . . it seemed so unfair! I had finally found happiness, and then to have it cruelly snatched away—'

Words shuddered up from Jewel's chest, in broken gulps. Words that had lain dormant in her heart for so long, growing in power, until they now erupted, released free into the world at last. She was shaken by their power.

'But how about me? Did I not make you happy?'

Now it was Evie's turn to look away. Whether in shame, or to hide the tears now trickling down her cheeks, Jewel couldn't tell.

'More than you know. Look at the name I gave you! You were so precious to me. But I was in no state to look after you properly . . . I turned up at Patricia's door in a terrible state one night.'

Jewel was vibrating with righteous rage. Yes, it was good to learn the story, to know the truth at last of who she was. Told by her own flesh-and-blood mother, not a clever piece of software. Yet no story ever told could change one fundamental, incontrovertible fact of her beginning.

'But. You. Abandoned me.'

Evie made no attempt to douse her daughter's fury. 'I did. You're right. I ran away. I did what I never should

312

have done. I returned to Folio chasing the past when I should have been nurturing the future. I don't expect you to forgive me. Yet.' She looked up, her eyes as red as Jewel's own. 'But I know this much. I'm so glad to see you again, daughter. And I want to know everything. Who you are, who you've become, what you've achieved.'

'I know now I'm never going to be the superhuman the green prince told me I was, a superior being, the next generation.'

'But you are, don't you see?'

'I'm just a girl, though.' Jewel wasn't expecting to feel so disappointed that she wasn't secretly a robot.

Evie took her by the shoulders, deadly serious. 'Now you listen to me, daughter. There is no such thing as *just a girl*. You came and rescued me, you brilliant girl!'

Jewel wasn't quite ready to forgive her yet. It wouldn't be that easy. Then again, what was? A small fire began to burn in her heart. There was one last question. 'So you weren't working on a new kind of being, a half human, half robot?'

'Of course! The prince, yet again, took a real truth and twisted it into a lie to torment you. I was developing someone very special.' Evie pointed to the figure behind her, collapsed in the shadows. 'You seem to have got on with her all right. Perhaps a few issues still to be ironed out.'

She gave a sheepish smile. Pandora bleeped feebly and tried to raise her left arm.

Jewel did a double take.

'But she—'

'Is amazing? I know.'

'Well,' said Jewel. 'She gets things wrong most of the time, sends us on terrible routes, can't tell jokes and . . .'

Her voice faltered as she realised the truth.

'And she saved your life?' said Evie.

Jewel nodded slowly. 'Yes, yes she did.'

'When I began to realise that the Stampstone was growing bad, controlling people rather than enabling them, I took some urgent precautions to protect Pandora from his grasp. I programmed her to appear more basic than she is so he would never suspect her as a threat. I hid her in open view. And I added one crucial instruction to her code.'

Jewel found herself looking at her battered assistant with a fresh wave of affection. 'What was that?' she said.

'To never harm a Reader or let any harm come to a Reader,' said Pandora, now sitting upright amidst the ferns. 'Which is why I will always be your best friend.'

Jewel remembered her appearing in the fairy ring,

leading them out of the Monster Marsh, helping her discover the invisibility cloak, rescuing her from the prince. And she began to think that, just possibly, a robot could be a kind of friend.

Then they all found themselves looking up, at the hole appearing in the tree canopy, as if it had been torn out of cloth. At the sun shining directly through it, blinding them at first, until the rays assumed something of a human form.

With a cape and slippers.

And offering a book.

'Perhaps,' said the Librarian, as he lightly landed in front of them, 'it is time to return home now.' He glowered at Evie. 'And never return!'

Evie nodded. 'I know. Forgive me. I should never have come back.'

'Never ever! You nearly destroyed the most precious world in existence.'

Evie took the book from him, her hand shaking. 'It's all right. I've paid my price. I'm afraid I will never be able to return, even if I wanted to.'

Jewel took her mother's arm. It was so thin. She wondered how much time they would have left together. That thought was too much to bear, so she focused on the book instead.

A slim, silvery grey hardback, a bit foxed at the edges.

The Silver Chair by C S Lewis.

'Oh! One of my favourites,' said Evie, turning it over in her hands.

'Is that Narnia? I'm not sure I've read that one.'

'You must! Once read, hard to forget.' She opened the book and gold steam began to curl up from the faded pages, just as it had at the Unicorn. 'But wonderful though it is, there are bigger adventures awaiting us both. At home. Which we have to face, whether we like it or not.'

Jewel gripped her mother's wrists. 'But what about Pandora? We can't just leave her?'

'You're not.'

The Librarian turned away from the pair, and pointed a glowing finger at the tottering robot. A beam of clear light shot out and encircled her. At first, nothing happened. Then her skin began to pulse, so gently, with delicate streams of numbers, and her eyes glowed the freshest blue they ever had. The Librarian kept on pointing, raising Pandora up into the air.

'Brave Unread,' he said, 'for your role in defeating the Stampstone prince and saving Folio, I do something no Librarian is ever meant to do.' He looked at Evie and

Jewel and arched an eyebrow. Was that even a tremble of a smile on his upper lip? 'I am reissuing you, with no fines payable.'

Sparks flew over Pandora's battered copper skin as she turned in the air, the scratches polished away into nothing, the dents flattening out, the numbers once more pulsing over the surface. She twisted, examining herself.

'It looks,' she said brightly, 'like you are looking for a new empress. May I help?'

'Yes, Pandora,' said the Librarian. 'You may. Will you restore order to this kingdom?'

'Would you like to order a cream bun?' said Pandora.

'There may be still one or two teething problems,' said Evie hastily.

Thumb coughed from the back of Majesty, bowing his head low to the Librarian. 'But . . . your Librarianship . . . I thought only Readers could rule in Folio?'

'Do not worry, fairy,' said the Librarian. 'They will be.' He turned to the robot. 'Pandora,' he said, 'show me your source code.'

Her blue eyes flickered and she raised her copper arm.

Jewel flinched in case she was about to fire her number ray, but instead, she projected a twirling beam of light, creating a film in the air. There was a flood of glowing numbers, equations, diagrams, and then . . . four heads, shining brightly in the early morning.

Jewel recognised them all.

Simon. Patricia. Evie. Larry. Her mother, uncles and aunt, the first Readers of Folio, reigning in perpetuity. Then, as she watched, another light-filled head joined the pantheon.

Her own.

The Librarian watched for a moment and then turned back to them. 'It is time for you all to return to your own world. But you will always be here, stored in Pandora's code, guiding her every decision. She may be a robot, but she was designed and built by a Reader. And in Folio, the most important rule has always been, and always will be—'

'Remember what you know,' said Thumb.

'Agreed,' said Jewel. 'But I'd like to add another of my own as well.' She looked around at the mother she had just discovered, the new friends forged in adventure, the world of ideas and stories that she would shortly leave behind . . . and realised that for the first time in her life, the dark shapes were no longer shifting and moving under the surface. There would be no more apologies at school for who she was, or hiding or running away when people tried to make her feel inferior to them.

Ever again. And she didn't even need the help of any technology.

Her face shone brightly, because, at last . . . she knew. 'Always remember who you are. Don't forget that, will you Pandora?'

Pandora nodded like a wise queen. 'Remember where you are!'

Everyone smiled at that, even the Librarian.

'Speaking of which,' said Jewel, 'I really would like to go home now, please.'

'Then you shall,' said the Librarian.

And there was just time for Thumb to clutch her finger tight, and for her to stroke Majesty a brief farewell, before Jewel and Evie were huddled tight around the old book.

'Is this the last chopper out of Saigon or what?' said Fizz at her feet. 'Room for a small one?'

'Always,' said Jewel, and she scooped him up, holding him close as Evie opened *The Silver Chair*, and the words began to disappear, along with the smiling Librarian, gleaming Pandora, Thumb, Majesty and all the fizzing bulbs and wonder of the Idea Jungle.

The golden clouds of the magical book enveloped them, beginning to draw them back to their own world. Invisible threads unfurled from the faded pages, wrapping themselves tight around the readers, drawing them further and further in . . .

Then they were falling into darkness, just as before.

But this time, rather than fighting it, Jewel closed her eyes, smiling. And allowed herself to dream about what might just, possibly, conceivably, happen the next time she walked into a bookshop . . .

1985 Jan 5th

Archive (TNA) (declassified 2019)

Private diary

When the Deputy Chief Scientific Adviser had concluded his presentation to the Cabinet, there was a stunned silence around the table. At length, the Prime Minister – as she so often did – broke the silence.

'Thank you for your presentation,' she said. 'It was most interesting. But are you seriously suggesting to this Cabinet that a disgraced former defence scientist, a former prisoner, no less, had not only discovered the means to access an alternate dimension, but having done so, encouraged children to explore it?'

There was a ripple of laughter in the room, but the Adviser remained stony faced. 'Prime Minister, all our witnesses were interviewed separately, without the opportunity for collusion. So unless they are the victims of a very ingenious hoax, or participating in mass hysteria—'

'Unless?' She sounded incredulous to the point of fury. 'And that in this . . . other universe, they discovered a black reflective stone which could somehow magically connect them to all the world's information all the time, stored on a computer network that over time learned so much from this information and how it was used, that the network itself grew more powerful than those who built and used the computers!' She made a gesture of sheer disbelief with her hands. 'And that ultimately, this database decided that it would be better for the world if it was run by computers rather than people.'

The Prime Minister shook her head in disbelief, as some of her colleagues offered smug smiles in agreement. 'I have heard some tall tales around this table' - more laughter - 'but really - magic stones, evil robots - this is the most incredible child's fantasy I have ever heard in my life.'

Still shaking her head, she closed the file in front of her. 'I don't think we need to be too worried...No one would ever believe it. You have retrieved all of Professor Kelly's files, and those of Evelyn Hastings?'

The adviser nodded.

'And these include working diagrams and detailed instructions on how to create such a computer network?'

He nodded again.

'Very well. You have our approval. Begin work immediately!'

END SECURITY FILE

ACKNOWLEDGEMENTS

"When you meet anything that is going to be
Human and isn't yet… or ought to be Human and
isn't, you keep your eyes on it and feel for your hatchet."
C.S. Lewis

Every story begins with another story, and stories in Folio
often begin with one that originated in Narnia. In 1984, as
a child, I read a powerful story of deceitful enchantment,
following a girl on a quest to an underground kingdom of
vivid, singular strangeness. The year I read *The Silver
Chair* was also the year I myself began a long enchantment
– which continues to this day – with technology, when our
family acquired our first personal computer. As we wrestle
with how the rapacious bewitchment of the digital
revolution has transformed our lives, for good and bad, it
seemed logical to return to the beginning – at least in my
imagination – and see where the story took me. I am

indebted once more to C.S. Lewis for firing the starting pistol, but also to Hannah Fry, James Bridle and Max Tegmark, amongst others, whose illuminating work on artificial intelligence and the future of an online connected world fills me with as much hope as it does trepidation.

This is the sixth book I have had the great privilege of working with Sarah Lambert on, as my editor, and I remain as grateful as ever for her patient, thorough, clear-headed and ever encouraging guidance. Not to mention that of her many equally supportive colleagues at Hachette Children's Group: Emily Thomas, Fiona Evans, Katherine Fox, Nic Goode, Ruth Alltimes, Anne McNeil and Hilary Murray Hill, who always make me feel part of the best publishing family.

When you build fictional worlds, it is all too easy to sometimes forget where you put things, and a profound thanks to Maurice Lyon for his forensic, scrupulous copy-edit, as well as Adele Brimacombe for her immaculate proofreading, both working with Rosie McIntosh who made the final production process as painless as it can be – and any remaining errors are mine.

I thought it would be hard for illustrator Ben Mantle and designer Samuel Perrett to outdo their work on *The Lost Magician*, but I now realise outdoing is what they do best – and still can't quite believe that I am allowed to have such a beautiful cover and artwork. They make Folio feel real, thank you both.

When I'm not writing, it is a joy of this job that I get to visit readers in schools all over the world, and the fact that I can still do that and find time to write is down to the supreme juggling skills of Victoria Rontaler – thank you for keeping me sane.

The children's author community is a generous and supportive one, and this past year I have been particularly grateful for the excellent company and very wise counsel of Abi Elphinstone, Lauren St John and Katherine Rundell – I salute you all.

Like those before them, this book would not exist without the tireless support of my indomitable agent Clare Conville, and my thanks to her and all her colleagues at C&W Agency, especially Allison DeFrees and Alexander Cochran.

But none of the above has to live with me while a book is written, and that dubious honour falls to Will Tosh and our dog Huxley. I love them both for many different reasons, but unfailing patience is pretty near the top of the list.

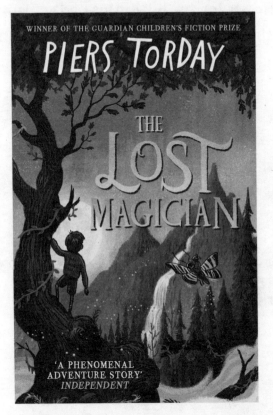

READ MORE AMAZING BOOKS BY PIERS TORDAY

Join Kester on his animal adventures in the bestselling and award-winning **THE LAST WILD** trilogy

And don't miss

A remarkable story about love, loss and the power of the imagination.